MARIE-HÉLÈNE LEBEAULT
AUTHOR OF THE EVERS SERIES

A SUMMER
— OF —
OPPOSITES
DEFENDERS OF THE REALM - NOVELLA TWO

BEACHES AND TRAILS
PUBLISHING

ABOUT THE AUTHOR

Marie-Helene Lebeault lives in Quebec, Canada and is the mother of two young adults. A retired teacher, she now spends her days writing, translating academic manuals, and lending her voice to corporate training videos. She enjoys reading, hiking, and going to the beach. She is also an avid rollercoaster fiend and is on a mission to visit all the Six Flags amusement parks with her daughter. Every year, she travels for three weeks on a solo adventure to a new part of the world.

Follow on Social Media, she'd love to hear from you!

Website Email Newsletter

facebook.com/mhlebeaultauthor

x.com/mhlebeault

instagram.com/mhlebeault

amazon.com/author/mhlebeault

bookbub.com/authors/marie-helene-lebeault

goodreads.com/mhlebeault

linkedin.com/in/mhlebeault

tiktok.com/@mhlebeaultauthor

youtube.com/@mhlebeault

ALSO BY THE AUTHOR

The Chronicles of the Starborne Cadets

Stars Beyond Realms

Shadows of Orion

Echoes of the Void

The Nebula's Heart

The Starborne Paradox

Defenders of the Realm

A Journey to Power

The Quest for the Emerald Rattleback

A Summer of Discovery

The Quest for the Sacred Tree

A Summer of Opposites

The Quest for the Phantom Feather

A Summer of Courage

The Quest for the Kraken's Ink

A Summer of Destiny

The Quest for the Cursed Mirrors

The Evers Series

The Ancestors' Key

The Academy

The Time Walker

The World Jumper

Blood Magick Trilogy

The Blood Mage

Blood Magick

Blood Legacy

Standalones

Clarity Castle

What Happens Next?

Ghost Stories

Holiday Shifters

Echoes of Tomorrow

Utopia

Picture Books

Fairy Grandmother: Millie Goes to Antarctica

Fairy Grandmother: Millie Goes to the North Pole

Fairy Grandmother: Millie Goes to China

Fairy Grandmother: Millie Goes to Africa

(Also available in French, Spanish, German, and Italian)

Editing by Rachael Lammie

Cover by Getcovers

ABOUT THE AUTHOR

Marie-Helene Lebeault lives in Quebec, Canada and is the mother of two young adults. A retired teacher, she now spends her days writing, translating academic manuals, and lending her voice to corporate training videos. She enjoys reading, hiking, and going to the beach. She is also an avid rollercoaster fiend and is on a mission to visit all the Six Flags amusement parks with her daughter. Every year, she travels for three weeks on a solo adventure to a new part of the world.

Follow on Social Media, she'd love to hear from you!
www.mhlebeault.com

Also by Marie-Hélène Lebeault

What Happens Next?

Ghost Stories

Holiday Shifters

Stranded with a Shifter

Dating a Shifter

Meeting the Shifters

Picture Books

Fairy Grandmother: Millie Goes to Antarctica

Fairy Grandmother: Millie Goes to the North Pole

Fairy Grandmother: Millie Goes to China

Fairy Grandmother: Millie Goes to Africa

(Also available in French, Spanish, German, and Italian)

CHAPTER

ONE

KAIA'S HANDS shook as she smoothed down her frilly frock. Was this too childish? She loves ribbons and ruffles, but maybe she should start wearing dresses that are sleeker.

The nerves that made her belly squish told her she needed a new dress. She was looking forward to this summer so badly! After the frankly exhausting school year she'd been through, she was eager to share a blissful summer with her fated mate.

Her fated mate.

The butterflies erupted again. Kaia still had the silvery threads that had bonded her and Nolen together tucked away safely in her nightstand. She and Nolen still had to decide what to do with them. Maybe they would bead them into two bracelets, the way her parents had. Or perhaps weave them into a blanket.

In any case, this summer was going to be fantastic. First, Nolen would come out to the schloss and get to know her family. Second, Kaia would go with Nolen to the Silent Marshes and join the Watch there, learning about Nolen's lifestyle and getting to know his family.

She and Nolen were already good friends. Kaia knew everything was going to work out easily. Her family would love him, and she'd love his family; how could it not work out? The Stars themselves chose them to be a perfect match.

Kaia pulled on a fresh dress and checked herself in the mirror. This one was more form-fitting, showing off her womanly figure. She thought that her body had finished its changes by this time; from the neck down, she looked almost exactly like Mama.

"I'm not ready to be a full-grown woman yet, though," she muttered as she pulled off the dress.

Outside her door, she could hear the shouts and playing of her massive extended family. All her aunts and uncles, and cousins had come to the schloss for the first bit of summer. They wanted to welcome Nolen into the family as well.

A knock came on her door. "Are you ready yet?"

That was Teresa, one of the little cousins. Technically, she was Kaia's second cousin twice removed, but who had the mental space to remember all that?

"I'm almost ready," Kaia called back.

Teresa whined. "I want to catch frogs!"

"We'll catch frogs tomorrow."

Kaia looked over the dresses she had pre-selected. No, none of them would do. Maybe she needed something less formal? She strode to the wardrobe and threw it open. It was bursting with the dresses Kaia had made over the last four months. She'd found that making clothing was quite a stress relief after a full day of studying and quickly spent all her money on the material to sew to her heart's content.

Now she wondered if she had gone a little overboard.

"Ah!" Kaia seized a blue checkered dress and pulled it out. Nolen had complimented this dress the first time she wore it. It was perfect!

"He's here!" a small voice shrilled from outside.

Thunderous cries echoed, and a stampede of feet sounded outside Kaia's door. She rushed to the window to see the carriage pull up. Her heart jumped to her throat. She wasn't ready yet!

She threw the dress on and quickly dampened her hair with water from the basin on her dresser. No time to style it, and brushing would just cause her curls to turn frilly. If only she hadn't wasted so much time on choosing the right dress! She didn't even have time to put on any makeup.

Shaking her head, she rushed from her room. By the time she got to the front door, the carriage was already clattering away, and Nolen was caught in a tight knot of her relatives, all introducing themselves at once.

Teresa seized Nolen's hand. "I wanna catch frogs!"

Kaia waded through her relatives to Nolen's side. He was standing tall and stiff, his expression grim. The sight shocked her, but she quickly dismissed the look. He was tired, that was all. She smiled warmly at him, and his lips twitched, but otherwise, he remained stoic as he pulled his hand away from Teresa.

"Give him space to breathe," Papa laughed as he shooed the relatives backward. "How was your trip, Nolen?"

"Fine."

Kaia glanced at his things. "Is this all?"

"Yes."

He had two canvas bags, one slightly larger than the other. How could this be enough for him to last two months?

"I'll show you to your room," Kaia grinned, reaching for the first bag.

Nolen shook his head. "I'll tent down by the lake."

Kaia straightened, frowning. "But we have a beautiful room for you all ready."

Nolen pulled his canvas bags over his shoulders. "I'd rather tent."

Kaia bit her lips together, fighting back her disappointment. If he were way out by the lake, they wouldn't be able to have spontaneous nighttime walks to look at the stars together like she hoped.

Aunt Greta leaned forward. "Oh, but if you're way out by the lake, how do you think you will join us for breakfast? We can't have someone running off after you every morning."

"I'm an early riser," Nolen said, his expression still stoic. "I doubt you will have breakfast early enough for me. I'll take care of my own food, thank you."

Several of Kaia's cousins glanced at each other. They had all been looking forward to another set of hands on the rotation roster. But if Nolen wasn't going to eat with them, he certainly wasn't going to be expected to cook or clean up with them.

Kaia had to fight back another wave of disappointment. Mealtimes were an important part of family get-togethers. She hated that Nolen was already giving her family a negative impression of him.

And why did he look so serious? Why wasn't he smiling?

She shook herself. "The lake is breathtaking," she said loudly as she gestured toward the path. "Let me show you the way—everyone else was just going to set up a game of pall mall, anyway."

As she started down the path, wondering if Nolen would comment on her dress when they were alone, Teresa bolted ahead of her.

"Yay!" the five-year-old cried. "Time for frogs!"

No!

"Frogs have delicate skin," Nolen said. "You shouldn't touch them. It's excruciatingly painful for them. The salt and sweat on our hands is like acid on their skin."

Teresa stopped, her eyes wide—then she burst into tears and raced back to her mother.

Why did he have to say it like that?

Kaia bit her tongue until they were at the lake. Finally, it was just the two of them. She turned to him, but he didn't look at her as he opened his bag and took out a tent.

"You're being rude," she blurted.

Nolen's head jerked up. "What?"

"We took a lot of time to clean out a room for you. And we like to have meals together; it's like you don't want to spend time with my family."

Nolen scowled as he put together the structure of the tent. "You can't expect me to spend every minute with your family, Kaia. I don't care about feather beds or giant breakfasts. If your family can't give me some space, they're the rude ones."

Kaia rocked back on her heels. That was the last thing she expected to hear, especially from Nolen! What was wrong that he was acting like this? He'd been here less than half an hour and already wanted nothing to do with her family.

Maybe this summer wasn't going to be magical after all.

Kaia folded her arms. "I get it. You're tired from your long journey and want to be alone."

"That's not what I said. I could use a little help to set up the tent, and then I'd like to go swimming."

Relief washed over her. Right! Nolen just didn't like to stand around talking. He liked to keep busy. "Excellent," she enthused. "I'll go get them to come help. Then we can play water tag!"

Nolen opened his mouth, but Kaia had already turned away. She skipped back up the path toward the schloss. This was going to be a perfect summer. She would make sure of it.

The End

If you enjoyed this book, please consider leaving a review on Goodreads, Bookbub, or your favorite retailer.

Reviews help me reach new readers.

Read *The Quest for the Phantom Feather*, the third book in the *Defenders of the Realm series!*

Join my newsletter at www.mhlebeault.com for writing updates, sneak peaks, review copies, sales, and giveaways!

CHAPTER

TWO

HOW DID Kaia have so many relatives? This was more like a hotel than a house. As if the sheer size of the mansion wasn't intimidating enough, there seemed like hundreds of people were there, all asking him the same questions over and over and over and over and over and over —

And over.

Nolen inhaled deeply as he approached the mansion—schloss— for the supper Kaia promised would be amazing. Normally in the Watch, everyone just ate when they were hungry. Feasts only happened on special days.

But maybe this special supper would finally just be him and Kaia alone together. He could understand if her family was concerned about leaving two sixteen-year-olds who had only recently learned they were fated mates alone together, but it was Kaia who kept bringing in other people. He didn't understand it. Didn't she want time to just sit and talk?

The conversation had been so easy between them over the last few years. Was Kaia secretly disappointed in him as her mate? Had he done something wrong so that she was ashamed of him?

As Nolen entered the schloss, the immediate noise set his teeth on edge. His shoulders tensed even as he fought back the reaction. Kaia's family was clearly important to her, and maybe there was still a chance that he'd be able to get to know them more naturally.

Rather than children throwing themselves at him and demanding he take them frog-catching or adults grilling him about his future plans.

To his shock and dismay, as Nolen made his way to the dining hall, he found it packed with no sign of Kaia... he could pick out her silver curls in this ocean of witches and dragons. Seriously, he had never heard of a single family being so prolific with non-humans before.

Tables lined the walls, laden with foods of every type. But why were they pushed up against the wall? The floor was open, with banners of silver and gold dripping from the ceiling—

Nolen's heart seized.

Oh, no.

Please no!

It was a dance.

He would have turned around and walked out right then, but Kaia had been so excited. He had to find her. If only her relatives wouldn't—

"Why, hello Nolen," at least five voices called in unison.

"How are you doing?"

"How's your day been?"

"Looking forward to the party?"

"Hope you have your dancing feet warmed up!"

Nolen picked his way through the sea of color and sound, trying desperately to figure out what questions were ones that needed answering and which weren't. So many people were talking to him all at once! And Kaia said he was rude?

There had to be more people in her family than the entire Watch, even when the various camps came together for training. His head pounded with the noise.

A man stepped in front of him. "Nolen, just the man I wanted to see."

Was this Kaia's father? No, Kaia's father had glowing silver eyes —this man was a witch with silver hair. Must be an uncle. "Yes, sir?"

The uncle laughed and slapped his back. "Your family is with the Swamp Watch, right?"

"Yes."

"How does that work for you? You got an excellent education, or were you always too busy moving around to learn properly?"

Nolen's lips pressed tightly together. What did it matter how he was taught? For that matter, his mother was trained to be a teacher. But how did this man he didn't even know have any right to demand such information?

"We were taught perfectly well," Nolen said, trying not to snap. "Frankly, it's insulting that you would think any differently."

"Whoa, there. I didn't mean—"

"You still said it," Nolen said. He narrowed his eyes at the uncle. "Unless you think a child has to have a multitude of tutors in order to be properly educated?"

An arm linked around his, and he nearly jerked it away, but it was Kaia. She tugged him away as she laughed at her uncle.

"You need to learn how to think before you talk," she called to him.

Her uncle laughed and waved a hand.

Nolen scowled. He was done with this. But Kaia was here now... maybe it would be better.

He took a moment to look at her. As usual, she was breathtaking. The sunshine yellow gown she wore matched her personality perfectly. She grinned at him, and some of the tension left his body.

Kaia always made him feel better. He smiled back.

"Want to dance?" she asked.

Nolen nodded once and pulled her into the dance floor. Most of it was occupied by kids running around and screaming, so he could hardly hear the music, but he focused on Kaia. She grinned at him, her eyes alight.

And if it was just the screaming kids, he might have been able to enjoy himself.

Unfortunately, it was the adults that ruined everything. They kept staring at him and Kaia, smiling at each other or whispering behind their hands.

What were they saying? Were they calling him a country bumpkin?

"Um, Nolen?" Kaia whispered.

He turned his attention back to her, stopping their dance. "What?"

"It's just that you were leading me in a foxtrot; this is a waltz."

Nolen's face flushed. He opened his mouth to explain that he couldn't hear the music, but that's not what came out. Because even if he could hear the music, he knew he wouldn't be able to lead her in a waltz... he couldn't remember the steps, even though they had dances with the Watch all the time after stressful days.

So instead of making an excuse that could lead to revealing this embarrassment, he scoffed and waved a hand. "Waltzes are boring."

Kaia blinked rapidly. She stepped back from him, and her cheeks burned red. "Oh. I guess it's not really for everyone. Maybe you'd like to do the tango? It's just that I'm not overly fond of the foxtrot."

Tango. How did someone dance a tango? Nolen tried to make his expression smooth, so she wouldn't see his misery.

From their first quest to the Silver Springs, he'd liked Kaia. She seemed so bright and cheerful. Panic welled in his chest. How was he supposed to match that energy? He wasn't made of sunshine like she was. Yellow, as good as it looked on her, was his least favorite color.

All he wanted to do was to pull her away from these hundreds of eyes. There might as well have been thousands of people here staring at him! They all could see he wasn't the mate that they wanted for Kaia.

"I'm done dancing," he said.

"Let's get some food, then." She pulled him toward the table.

Dozens of forks met his eye. Kaia selected a delicious-looking meat pie and handed it to him. Nolen stumbled as he grabbed up the nearest fork.

"No, that's for dessert," Kaia said.

Nolen dropped the fork and put the pie down. As attracted as he was to Kaia, he really didn't know her. The time they had spent together up to now had always been intruded upon by one thing or another. How was he supposed to get to know her here when there were too many people and too many forks?

"Here, this one," Kaia said, picking up a fork that looked almost exactly the same as the one he'd had before. "And I can teach you how to waltz if you want."

Nolen shook his head. "I'm not hungry. And I know how to waltz. I just don't like it. I wasn't expecting a party. I only came because I didn't want to be rude. I'm tired. I'm going back to the lake."

"Nolen," Kaia protested, her eyes widening.

He really couldn't stand to be here any longer. If he didn't get away from the noise and staring, he was going to rip out his own hair! It wasn't fair that Kaia told him it was going to be special and then to ambush him with all her family again!

Without another word, Nolen power-walked from the dining hall, then ran all the way back to the lake. His stomach rumbled as he threw himself into his tent.

Guilt and frustration warred inside of him. So many people he had to impress.

But he didn't want to impress any of them.

He just wanted to get to know his mate... was that so terrible?

CHAPTER

THREE

KAIA PULLED on a shawl to go after Nolen, her face flaming red. He just booked it out of there as though his tail was on fire! Had she really messed up that badly by offering to teach him to waltz?

Maybe she shouldn't have assumed that he didn't know how, but Kaia would never have thought he would react this way.

As she headed for the front door, however, Mama and Papa found her. Kaia drew up to a stop, wishing they had stayed in the ballroom. She made herself smile at them, not wanting them to realize anything was wrong. But judging by the expressions on their faces, they already knew.

"Aunt Mixie said she saw Nolen leave in a hurry," Mama said. "Is everything all right?"

"Oh, he was feeling a little sick and tired from the trip," Kaia said quickly, waving a hand. She held up a basket of bread. "I was just going to take him some food and see if he needed anything."

Mama and Papa gave each other a look. Kaia flushed deeper, blinking rapidly. But luckily, they didn't question her further.

The tent was quiet when she arrived with the basket, and when she called out to Nolen, she only got a grunt in response.

"I brought you some food," she said, standing outside the tent. "I'll just leave it here."

She put it on the ground and hurried away, tears pricking at her eyes. So, he was still awake but didn't even talk to her. He'd rather be by himself than spend any time with her, it seemed. Her hands clenched into fists as she made her way back to the schloss.

Once there, she returned to the dance so she could give the appropriate excuses for Nolen before claiming exhaustion herself.

She retreated to her room and changed into a nightgown, then sat at her window as she wrapped her short curls in ribbons to keep them from tangling too badly during the night. A small flicker of light out by the lake showed Nolen had started a fire.

Maybe he was embarrassed because he couldn't dance. Maybe she shouldn't have corrected him about that stupid fork. It wasn't a big deal; she didn't have to babble about it being wrong for meat pie. Maybe he really was feeling tired, and he'd been asleep when she went to the tent.

Maybe.

She rubbed her eyes. "Tomorrow will be better," she told herself firmly. "We'll all have a good sleep and have lots of energy for everything we have planned."

And with that, she lowered the blind and moved to her bed, laying over the covers as the night was still warm from the day. Tomorrow would be better. She was determined it would be.

THE NEXT MORNING, she dressed in a white dress with ruffles at the hem and put on a matching hat before she made her way to the lake. Nolen was already awake. He had a neat little camp set up, with a clothesline strung with the shirt he'd worn yesterday hanging up to dry. Dishes sat nearly stacked on a folding table, drying in the sunlight.

"Morning," she called as she approached.

Nolen, who was sitting at the edge of his tent and writing in a notebook, looked up. He looked more relaxed and rested than he had the previous night. Good.

"We're all heading into town," she told him, grinning. He didn't know it, but it was a tradition for the newest mate brought into the family to be heaped with gifts on the first excursion into town. "We'll be leaving in an hour."

Nolen's brows knit together. "What?"

"Town. We're going to do some shopping and—"

"Who is *we*?" Nolen interrupted. His expression was closed-off.

Kaia felt herself tensing, though she fought it. "All of us. The whole family. And you, of course."

"I don't want to go into town. What am I going to do there?" Nolen scowled as he slid a marker into his notebook and shut it. "I've got work to get done. That dock your cousins were using yesterday needs to be repaired. Eventually, someone's going to get splinters."

Kaia folded her arms. "But this is tradition. Whenever someone gets a new mate, the family takes them to town. We go shopping, and at the end of the day, we have a meal at the theater while watching a play. We already have the reservations."

"Can't we just go for the meal and the play?" Nolen's scowl deepened.

"No! That's not how we do things. I told you about this before we left the Institute," Kaia snapped, unable to stop herself. She narrowed her eyes at him. "If you didn't want to—"

"I thought you were talking about you and your parents, not the entire family tree." Nolen scrubbed his hands over his eyes. "Okay, fine. If it's that important to you, I'll come."

"Try not to sound so enthusiastic. We're not going to torture you." Kaia tightened her arms.

"I said I'd come, Kaia."

Kaia let out a heavy breath, trying to release her annoyance. He was coming, and that was what was important. Once they were in town and he started getting the gifts, he'd change his tune. She had so much to show him in town! It was going to be perfect.

·ﻬ·

THIS WAS the worst day of her life. Nolen hadn't smiled once since they got into town. He walked by her and nodded every once in a while as Kaia told him about the sights, but he didn't respond with more than one word at a time. Whenever anyone else tried to get him to open up, it was even worse!

What was going on?

He wasn't even accepting any of the gifts, only stating that it wasn't something he personally would use, no matter what it was. When Aunt Mixie tried to buy him a handsome new scarf, Nolen told her he had never used a scarf anyway, so it would only be a waste of money.

During the small moments when she took some time away from him, she still noticed he didn't engage with her family at all. More than one of her cousins told her over the course of the day that they didn't think he liked them.

By the time supper and the play were over, Kaia was more than happy to go home. She was miserable and unable to keep any sort of mask up anymore. All she'd wanted was a perfect day, and Nolen couldn't even be bothered to realize that everyone was offering him gifts for a reason.

When they returned to the schloss, he immediately stated he would go back to his tent. Kaia walked with him.

"It's fine, you don't have to come with me," Nolen told her, his voice strained.

He was angry? *He* was angry? He'd just ruined the most important day of the summer, and he was angry?

"Hey." Kaia's voice was sharper than she wanted, but she was too upset to care. "What is wrong? You've been acting like we were marching you to the gallows all day!"

"Nothing is wrong," Nolen replied. His voice was sarcastic as he added, "Except apparently, the only thing that makes you happy is to have a million people around you all the time. A million people who can't shut up for two seconds and who are always pushing and poking and asking question after question! If I have to tell one more of your cousins that yes, I'm on the Swamp Watch, I'll lose it."

This wasn't what she wanted.

And the anger welling through her only made it worse. They were already fighting; she didn't want to make it worse. So, she turned around and started back to the schloss. If she said anything else, she was going to yell.

Kaia hated being angry. She hated being upset with someone else.

But why would he talk that way about her family? It was like he didn't even want to get to know them! He was a grumpy, cold island, and it seemed like he wanted to stay that way.

Kaia took the back stairs to avoid everyone as she went to her room. The last thing she wanted was for them to see her so upset because of her mate. This was supposed to be a perfect match, and yet they were only two days into the summer, and so far, everything that happened just showed that they weren't a good match, let alone perfect.

She had been so happy when she realized Nolen was her fated mate. She had felt the perfection between them.

How could she have been so wrong?

CHAPTER

FOUR

TWO WEEKS OF PURE MISERY. Just how long were all of Kaia's family members going to be around? She never talked about them hanging out for so long. Didn't any of them have jobs?

Nolen tried. He really did. He tried to be polite and to calmly deflect the multitude of questions directed at him. He tried to be gracious about turning down everything they tried to force on him. How many times did he have to say that he liked his clothes just fine before they stopped buying him new shirts?

He knew what they were really doing. They thought something was wrong with how he dressed and were trying to make him more 'suitable.' He had heard from Icarus how in Odentia, people with lower incomes were looked down on, but he'd never thought it would happen in Eldavon. At least, not until now.

Even swimming wasn't enjoyable since there were at least a dozen cousins making a racket at any given time.

All Nolen wanted was some quiet, alone time with Kaia, where they could actually talk. But he couldn't even compliment her dress without a crush of other people piling on to give their opinions too!

He was lying in his tent, staring up at the light, peering through the canvas, and missing the Silent Marshes with their peace and quiet terribly when he heard soft footsteps approaching. He tensed. Which cousin was going to come berate him now?

"Nolen?"

He rolled to a sitting position, heart in his throat. Kaia!

"Are you awake?" she asked near the front of his tent.

"Yes," he called back, quickly tidying up. "Just a minute!"

He pulled a shirt on over his head and straightened his bedroll. As he combed his fingers through his hair, he went to the door flap and pulled it open.

Kaia looked stunning in a flowy lilac sundress. Nolen welcomed her inside, and she took a seat on one of the folding chairs he had brought. She folded her hands on her knees, looking around everywhere except for him.

"Can we talk?" she asked eventually.

"Yes. What's on your mind?"

Kaia chewed her lip, avoiding his eyes. "Well... it's just that you haven't been acting like yourself. At the Institute, you're much more... what I mean is... you've been acting withdrawn and distant. So, I was just wondering... I mean, it feels like I'm doing something wrong, but I don't know what that is."

Nolen flinched. Of course, Kaia would see that things weren't right. He opened his mouth, intending to tell her that the problem was he was completely overwhelmed—but he stopped himself. Her family was clearly important to her.

How could he tell her that the problem was that they were always there every moment of the day? He had tried to drop hints before that he felt pressured by the sheer amount of people around, but it wasn't the same as telling her he didn't want her family around.

Certainly not because they were being judgey toward him and always trying to make him change under the guise of gifts.

This was normal life for her. She wouldn't understand where he was coming from.

"I knew it." Kaia's shoulders slumped forward. "It's because I forced you to go to town, isn't it? You didn't want to, and I forced you to, and you're still upset about it."

"What? No!"

"Then why?" Kaia stared at him pleadingly.

Nolen sucked in a deep breath, trying to figure out how to word this in a way that wouldn't upset her further. "I'm used to being at the Silent Marshes. It's very... noisy here. I'm not used to having so much to listen to all at once."

Kaia's brows furrowed.

"And... and I know that they're your family and they're concerned about you, but I don't like how they're always asking me a million questions," he continued, talking rapidly now. Maybe if he just blurted it out? "It feels like I'm in an inquisition, and I can't keep up with it all."

"What sort of questions?"

Nolen flushed. She'd think he was stupid. "Honestly? Asking me about my parents, about Odele, about how my schooling is going. It's just constant, and even things like 'how did you sleep last night' are asked repeatedly."

He watched her closely, hoping to see the understanding on her face. But she only looked more confused than ever.

"They're just being polite."

"That's the thing—I don't find it polite. It feels rude to be heaping questions on me like that."

"But it's not."

"To *you*," Nolen said, exasperated. "Not to me! It's not normal in the Watch. We know how to mind our own business."

Kaia's shoulder slumped. "Oh. That's why you've been acting so weird these last couple of weeks."

He didn't think he was being weird, more like reacting normally to the sheer force being thrown at him. He didn't say that, though, and instead just nodded.

"Maybe it will be better if you join us for game night, then?" Kaia asked, leaning forward. "I can sit with you and tell them all to stop asking so many questions."

Nolen let out a ragged sigh of frustration. "No, game night won't be helpful, Kaia. There are too many people for me. It's too noisy. I can't hear myself think. I don't know how to be any plainer about this!"

"But they're my family."

"I know. But I can't just change how I am. I don't do well with piles of people around, even when I know them. It's too much." Nolen leaned forward, fixing her with his gaze. He wanted so badly for her to understand where he was coming from!

Kaia rubbed her temples. "How are you supposed to get to know them if you refuse to spend any time with them?"

"Kaia," Nolen complained, leaning back again. "I can't get to know them when there's a million of them around all the time."

"You haven't even tried."

Nolen got to his feet. "I'm thirsty. Let's get some water."

Kaia got to her feet, looking upset. Nolen hated that he was the reason she looked like that, but it was like everything he said. She heard something else. Was he the one saying things wrong, or was she hearing it wrong?

After they both got some water, the two walked around the lake. Nolen kept expecting her to just walk away and remained tense. How was he supposed to express himself? Back home, he had never had this much trouble. Odele and his parents seemed to always understand what he was trying to say when he wasn't being clear.

Right now, he thought he was being clear. There were too many people, and he needed space. He didn't know anyone here, not even Kaia. Yes, he knew her better than anyone else here at the schloss, but that didn't mean he actually knew her.

"What are you thinking?" he finally asked.

"I don't know," she mumbled, turning her face away.

That was the sort of thing that Odele did when she was angry with him. Nolen tensed up again. What had he done to make Kaia mad at him? He was just trying to be honest! He never said he didn't want to get to know her family, only that there were too many people all at once.

They walked around the lake, both quiet. Nolen wanted to break the silence between them but couldn't find the words. He'd messed this all up and didn't know how to fix it.

They got back to his tent to find the entire army of Kaia's family at the lake. They splashed about, yelling and cheering and laughing. Nolen's body tensed up so much his back hurt. What were they doing here? Normally when they were at the lake, they were at least down the shore, not right at his safe spot.

"Kaia, Nolen!" one aunt called, waving them over. "We saw you two were missing and brought the fun to you. Kaia, run and get your swimsuit on. We're going to be here for a while."

No.

No! This was his space to get away from the noise. If he went inside, how many would follow? Why couldn't they just leave?

The pressure rose in his chest.

Kaia laid her hand on his arm. "We could have a good time—"

Nolen ripped his arm away. His temples throbbed as he turned on her. Had she set it up? Had she told them to come hang out here, thinking that if she forced him to spend time with them, he'd like them?

"Don't tell me we could have a good time," he yelled, far too aware of the many eyes on him. He couldn't hold it in, though, no matter how much he wanted to. "I've told you again and again that it's too many people! I thought the summer was about us getting to know each other, but every time I turn around, I'm being ambushed by yet another relative! Stop pushing them on me!"

One uncle started forward. "Whoa. Calm down there. What's happened?"

Nolen whirled around, his vision glazed with the anger and frustration that he was, even now, ashamed to let erupt. "Stop asking me questions!" he yelled. "Leave me alone for two seconds so I can hear myself think!"

He marched toward his tent, trembling as silence finally descended. He shut the door and packed up his things.

There. He said what he wanted to say.

And he'd just completely blown it.

CHAPTER
FIVE

KAIA BURIED her face in her pillow, muffling the sound of her sobs.

She had never seen Nolen so angry. She thought that if everyone was at the lake, where he was most relaxed, her family would finally see the true him. She never thought that he'd end up blowing up at her like that.

Too many people. How could it be too many people? There were more people at the Institute than there were in her family! He hadn't even given them a chance.

Hadn't given her a chance.

Maybe he didn't want her for his mate after all. Maybe he wanted to be a swamp hermit, and he was angry that she would never want to have that sort of life? It was ridiculous; she knew it wasn't true, and yet her mind kept getting crueler and crueler, both to her and Nolen.

Of course, he'd think her family was too much when he barely spoke to anyone at all.

Of course, she'd mess this up when she couldn't think about anyone other than herself.

Of course, of course, of course.

A knock sounded on her door. "Go away!"

"Kaia, it's Heather."

"Go away!"

But Heather didn't go away. Instead, she opened the door and came in. "You don't have to talk to me, but I think you need to listen."

Kaia pulled her blanket over her head, hiding from Heather's sight. Maybe it was immature for a sixteen-year-old to do, but she had already told her to go away twice, and she wasn't listening.

Heather sighed, and the creaking of the chair next to Kaia's desk told her she had sat down.

"I know that you're feeling awful and embarrassed right now," Heather said. "You feel you messed up or Nolen messed up. Or even that the Stars messed up. I know. I had those same thoughts when Gregory first introduced me to the family."

Gregory was the last cousin to have been a dragon. Heather was his witch-match.

"The family is a lot to get used to. When you grow up in a clan as tight-knit as this, it's easy to lose perspective. Nolen is part of the family now, but he hasn't always been. It's only natural that he gets overwhelmed to start with. He seems like a very serious type, and he has a point about wanting to get to know you without the pressure of an audience."

"He didn't have to blow up like that," Kaia said into her pillow.

"Maybe not," Heather agreed. "But have you really sat down to talk with him?"

"I tried."

The chair creaked, and the mattress sagged slightly. "I know it's hard, Kaia. The thing about being sixteen is that you're in a weird place where you're becoming more self-aware while still figuring out what you actually are. Give him some grace. Let him apologize. And Kaia? Give yourself grace, too."

Kaia pulled her blanket tighter and was silent. Give herself grace? What was that supposed to mean? She remained silent as Heather left; once she was gone, Kaia threw back the blankets and hurried to the door, which she locked.

Then she went back to her bed and crawled underneath it. It was slightly cooler in the dark, and Kaia laid her head on her arms.

What was she going to do now?

***

OVER THE NEXT FEW DAYS, all her cousins slipped away, family by family. A few of them left some gifts for her and Nolen, but most just quietly left. Kaia couldn't stop herself from feeling utterly humiliated by all of this.

If she had listened to Nolen earlier, would things have fallen apart like this?

If he had just been clearer in what he needed to say, that he wanted time alone with her rather than saying there were too many people, would that have changed anything?

Maybe she should have told him more about her plans for the summer. It never occurred to her he'd oppose to any of her family traditions... and it never occurred to her they would actually make him angry.

How could she keep him in her life if he didn't want her family in it, too? They were a package deal.

Was he thinking about breaking their mate bond?

Only one thing was clear to her. Her family was no longer at the schloss, and instead of having a joyous welcome addition to the family, Nolen hated them. And they had a terrible impression of him, too. What was she supposed to do with this now? How could she come back from it?

She had no idea.

Even after her family was gone, though, Nolen didn't seem to want to spend time with her. She sometimes went down to the lake and walked around the familiar path, hoping he'd join her. He never did. If he came to the schloss, she never saw him.

"I feel like I've lost everything," she told Mama one night in the parlor.

Kaia's eyes flooded with tears as she twisted her head away. Mama should have gone back to work by now. Summer was the busiest time of year for agriculturalists, after all. Now her relationship drama was spilling over into other areas of life, and random people she didn't even know were suffering for it.

"Honey, have you tried talking to him again?"

Kaia scowled. "If he wanted to talk, he'd come to me. He hasn't even apologized for yelling at me!"

Mama sighed. "That is a problem, I'll grant you. But just think for a moment. Maybe the reason he hasn't apologized is that you're clearly avoiding him, and he doesn't want to push his presence on you?"

"I'm not avoiding him."

"Then how come every time we hear the door open, you immediately jump up and run to your room?"

Kaia rubbed her eyes. She wanted to say she didn't do that, but she had to admit... she really did. And thinking about it, Nolen didn't even know where her room was. "But he could write me a note."

"And you could write him a note."

Kaia turned a glare at her mother. "I'm not the one who caused all the problems! He's the one who yelled at me in front of everyone. He's the reason everyone left. Why should I attempt to talk if he won't? I tried to do that before, and he still didn't tell me what was really bothering him."

Mama shook her head. "I can't give you all the answers, Kaia. I'm only saying what helps when your father and I fight."

"You and Papa don't fight."

Mama laughed. "Oh, if only that were true! We don't argue the way we used to, no, but it hasn't always been smooth sailing between us."

Kaia had to roll her eyes at that. She knew a lie when she heard it. "You and Papa are perfect together."

"Far from it. Perfection isn't possible, Kaia. Talk about your expectations and communicate." Mama shook her head. "Expecting perfection is a recipe for disaster."

As she stood and moved to the window, she pondered her mother's words. Was she expecting too much from Nolen? Should she be the one to seek him out? Or maybe he was the one who needed space. Maybe she needed to stay away and let him figure himself out.

She rested her forehead against the glass.

She still didn't know what to do. If anything, she was more confused than ever... so what was she going to do?

CHAPTER
SIX

DAWN WAS BARELY PEEKING over the eastern mountain as Nolen crept into the schloss. Kaia's father, Charles, had given him a key to the schloss so he could come and eat as he saw fit. Charles had also told him that if he needed to talk, either he or Kaia's mother, Lacey, would hear him out, judgment-free.

Since his blowup at Kaia and her family, though, he was far too embarrassed to show his face at the schloss. Kaia had to hate him now. From the lake, he'd seen her relatives leave.

It was all his fault. Because instead of telling her upfront what the problem was and working with her to sort out the problem, he held it in until he ended up screaming at her and everyone else. That wasn't okay.

Now, he was counting down the days until he returned to the Silent Marsh. The only thing he didn't know was if Kaia would come with him.

But if she hadn't ambushed me with so many relatives all at once, none of this would have happened.

Nolen shook his head, trying not to fall into a pattern of blame as he lit the stove. He'd cook his food and then get to work. He had fixed up the dock by this time, but there was more work to be done around the grounds. There were an awful lot of bushes on the path around the lake that needed to be cleared out.

Kaia often walked around the lake, especially at twilight. She must get caught on the burrs; she'd have an easier time if they were gone.

He cooked as he planned out his day. As he turned to find the dishes, though, he nearly jumped out of his skin.

Madame Adora, Kaia's language tutor, stood behind him. She was a stately woman with long hair and, right now, a rather stern expression on her face.

Until Kaia had introduced him to Madame Adora, it hadn't occurred to him that Kaia was still learning different languages.

"Hello," he mumbled, averting his eyes.

"Hello," Madame Adora responded. She held something out toward him. "I found this feather while walking around the grounds yesterday and was wondering if you, with your experience in the Silent Marsh, could identify what bird it came from."

Nolen cleared his throat and took his food off the burner before he inspected the feather. "Looks like it's from a blue jay."

"But it's not blue. How can you tell?"

Nolen took the feather and turned it back and forth so the light caught it. "See the banded patterns? You don't really find that in other birds. So, my guess is that it's got a mutation or something that makes it darker than normal."

Madame Adora took the feather back, then held out a pretty pink flower. "I see. And this flower, what sort is it?"

"Looks like a ranunculus."

"Not a rose?"

Nolen shook his head. "See the leaves? These are much more

fern-like, while roses are smooth and hard. And the flower has no scent. Ranunculus, not a rose."

Madame Adora nodded again and tucked her hands into her robe. "And how are you finding the grounds? Are you getting enough rest in your tent?"

Nolen turned quickly away and dished out his food. "It's fine."

"Hmmm." She tapped her chin as she studied him in a way that made the hair on Nolen's arms prickle. The intense concentration made him feel like she was about to declare his execution. Eventually, she nodded and looked away. "I thought so."

"You thought what?" Nolen grabbed silverware and took his plate to the table.

Madame Adora gathered herself up some fruits. "Everyone has been talking about how reserved and rude you've been. I thought that couldn't be right. The Stars wouldn't align sunshiny Kaia with a rude boy."

Nolen hunched his shoulders. He was right. They did all think he wasn't worthy of her.

"But it seems to me that you're just shy when talking about yourself," Madame Adora continued. "Goodness knows this family doesn't know what shy means. They think it's when you have too many butterflies to think clearly. They don't understand the anxiety."

Nolen winced. Shy was not a word he liked, no matter how true it was.

"Why haven't you told Kaia that you're shy?"

"She knows I'm shy."

Madame Adora gave him an unconvinced look.

"She does," Nolen insisted. How could she not? She should understand that his aversion to crowds and people wasn't just because he didn't like her family specifically.

"I have another question for you, Nolen," Madame Adora said, folding her arms.

Nolen ground his teeth. Always more questions! "Yes?"

"Do you want to make things work with Kaia? Do you want her to be your fated mate?"

But she already was his fated mate. Anxiety rose in his throat. Was this a roundabout way to tell him that Kaia no longer wanted him? Was she looking into breaking the bond?

His answer was strangled, "Of course, I do!"

"Then you need to communicate. First, apologize for yelling. Then, work on sharing with her how you feel, even if it will upset her. Don't just bottle things until you explode." Madame Adora nodded once and headed for the door. "I heard her moving around her room before I came down. I advise you to go talk to her right now before you get too deep into that head of yours and overthink things."

She headed away, grumbling. "All these witches and dragons expecting relationships to magically happen. Just because you have magic, doesn't mean that it works that way." She paused in the doorway and turned back, pointing a finger at Nolen. "That's one thing humans certainly learn! A relationship takes work. Just because you are each other's perfect matches doesn't mean you're automatically perfect."

She left the kitchen then.

Nolen turned her words over in his head as he slowly ate. She had a point... he hadn't really been communicating his needs to Kaia except in outbursts. Even then, how was Kaia supposed to know the root cause of it when all he said was that there were too many people and too many questions?

As he reflected on his behavior, he winced. If someone had come to him with these complaints about Odele and his parents, he would think it was something personal.

He had to figure out how to make this right.

Interrupting Kaia's sleep somehow didn't feel like the right call, though.

Madame Adora advised him not to overthink, but Nolen wasn't sure exactly what that meant. The only times he didn't think things through before he acted, he ended up making them worse. Surely it was better to give his problem some serious thought and come up with a good plan of action?

And he had just the thing!

Kaia's favorite cake was vanilla with buttercup frosting. She'd told him about it last semester on her birthday. There had to be a recipe around here somewhere...

He searched the cupboards and finally found the recipe books. It took him a while, but he discovered a recipe for vanilla cake. Though he couldn't find anything for buttercup icing, he'd figure out that later.

Several hours later, Kaia came into the kitchen, rubbing her eyes. She stopped when she saw him putting the finishing touches on the cake.

"Oh. I can come back," she mumbled, then turned.

"Wait." Nolen pushed the cake toward her. He wanted to tell her he'd made it for her because he knew he had ruined her plans, but suddenly his tongue felt like it was tied in a knot. Everything he'd planned to tell her went right out of his head.

Kaia came back, staring at the cake. "It's got roses on it."

"I couldn't find buttercups."

"Oh." A moment of silence. "Is it for me?"

Nolen nodded. "Sorry for yelling."

"You didn't have to make a cake to say sorry."

Nolen nodded but found he couldn't look at her. He needed to say more, but everything that came to mind just sounded like an excuse. What could he say? He took a deep breath, held it, then released it in a big rush.

"Are you still coming to the Silent Marshes?" he blurted.

Kaia turned his cake around, her expression guarded. "Do you want me to?"

"Yes. Please."

Kaia finally looked up. Her expression was set and calm. "I think I will. But only if my parents agree to come as well."

Nolen repressed a flinch. It made sense why she'd want her parents to come along in case she wanted to leave again. It would be easier for her to get away from him if she had her parents' support right there.

He nodded. "That'll be good. Having your parents there. They'll... they'll enjoy it, too."

And, without knowing what else to say, he quickly escaped from the kitchen. As he headed back to his tent, he couldn't help but berate himself. Why couldn't he just say what he wanted to say? Madame Adora was right... communication was important. So then, why did his brain forget all his words when he was around Kaia?

CHAPTER
SEVEN

KAIA GROANED as she looked at herself in the mirror. She was an absolute mess! Not only were there dark circles under her eyes from her lack of sleep but also her hair was in knots. It was going to take forever for her to be presentable again.

She and her parents had been in the camp for the Watch for three weeks now. At first, she didn't think it would end up being a big deal that she forgot a few of her haircare essentials; she thought it would be easy enough to just go to town and pick them up.

Only it was half a day's journey to get to the nearest town. Which meant every time anyone went to town, it was an overnight trip.

And then, every few days, they packed up camp and moved to a new location, which meant she had taken the vast majority of the things she'd brought back to town and paid for storage until she went back home. There were also no baths. You had to haul the water and heat it up... even the camps she'd been on for schooling hadn't been this difficult.

Why hadn't someone figured out an easier living by now?

Herja's bookbag could have come in handy. They'd be able to carry twice as much with only a fraction of the weight on their backs.

"Kaia," Nolen called from outside the tent. He sounded full of energy. "Are you ready?"

Kaia sighed and tied a scarf over her hair to hide it, then pulled on a simple smock. She had foolishly only brought one pair of trousers, and they were currently hanging up to dry after she had fallen into a slime pit.

She came out of the tent. "As ready as I can be," she grumbled.

Nolen smirked at her. If there was one good thing about coming to the Silent Marshes, it was that there was an obvious change in Nolen at once. Even though he had hoped that Adina and Odele would be here, he and Odele could introduce some of his favorite games to Kaia.

Instead, his twin sister and her mate were spending the summer with Adina's family. Since Adina's parents were the human king and queen of Eldavon, she had many responsibilities to the Kingdom as well.

"You're beautiful," he told her, grinning widely. "I never noticed before how much makeup you wear."

Kaia blushed as she touched her cheek. "I like makeup."

Nolen nodded. "I know, but I didn't realize how much. You have an artistic hand for sure, especially that little loop you do with your eyeliner. But you are beautiful, no matter what is or isn't on your face."

"Thanks." She stretched her arms over her head. "So, what's on the docket for today? Is the rest of your family coming soon?"

Nolen's brows pinched together. "Odele is spending the summer with Adina."

Kaia frowned back at him. "I know that. I mean the rest of your family. Aunts, uncles, cousins...?"

Nolen looked away, a faint shadow on his face. "Nobody else is coming. Like I told you at the schloss, I thought the summer was about us getting to know each other, not our families. I didn't invite anyone to the Watch. Besides, they're all busy with work."

"But they could take time off," Kaia protested as she followed him toward the mess tent. "The Crown makes sure that everyone has enough—"

"Kaia." Nolen stopped and held up both his hands. "I didn't want them to come."

She pinched her lips tightly together. Yes, she understood him finding her family overwhelming—now—but he didn't invite any of his extended relatives? Not even Odele was here? Did that mean that he didn't want her to meet them?

Was she not important enough to shove off his discomfort of crowds?

Kaia shook her head. No. He wanted time together, just the two of them. Although, with all the work they had been doing lately, it wasn't like they had had much time with just the two of them, anyway!

Quit whining, she told herself sharply. *You have to make an effort here, too; you know.*

"I cooked up some sausages and eggs," Nolen said as he dished out a large plate.

Nobody else was in the tent, which meant he cooked them just for her. Kaia smiled as she took a seat. She had to admit; she did like it when it was just the two of them. Even when it was just her parents around, Nolen got quieter and didn't talk as much.

At least his parents and hers got along well. They talked easily with each other and seemed to be keen to make suggestions for each other's work. Mama got super excited when Nolen's father suggested using some of the swamp-tending techniques on the floodlands. They were making tentative plans to work together after summer, too.

"We're cleaning out a bunch of old brush today," Nolen said as he slid into the seat next to her. "You're going to want long sleeves."

Kaia's appetite died. More physical labor. She had never thought she minded hard work, but as it turned out, she really didn't know what hard work was.

She sighed as she rested her chin on her hand. "You'd think that I got used to gathering wood during the Institute's camps. It never seemed like that big of a deal when we were keeping fires going."

"It's different when you're only gathering enough for a single night," Nolen said, his tone sympathetic. "The work never stops in the Watch. We have a heavy responsibility here."

No time to just relax, it seemed. "But when do you take time for your studies?"

"School is all year. Why should I have to spend my summer with my nose in a book, too?" Nolen asked.

Kaia poked at a sausage. Then, seeing Nolen's expression fall, she cut into it. "This looks delicious. Cooked perfectly."

It wasn't; it was a little burned. But Nolen had cooked them for her himself, and that made up for a bit of burned edges. She smiled at him as she ate. She had to admit even if she didn't like the intensive physical labor here; the Watch kept it fun. There was always singing and stories of some sort.

"Do you think tonight we could take a walk through the marshes?" she asked as Nolen cleaned up—without even waiting for her to be finished, which made her rush.

"Why? We'll be working all day in them," Nolen replied with a laugh.

"I want to look at the stars."

Nolen's brow furrowed. "I don't think that'll be a good idea. You look like you haven't been sleeping well, and it doesn't get dark enough to see the stars until late; we're going to be moving again tomorrow, so you should get a good sleep tonight."

Kaia bit back her disappointment. "All right," she said.

Moving again. Working all the time. When were they going to have fun? Hadn't Nolen made any plans for while she was here other than continuing with the same day-in, day-out routine?

She tried not to feel disappointed about this. Maybe he was saving it up for something special later. But she was disappointed. She just wasn't sure how to tell Nolan that she needed something... *more.*

CHAPTER
EIGHT

NOLEN WAITED OUTSIDE of the tent Kaia's family slept in, bouncing on his toes with impatience. They had little time, but from the groggy conversation Kaia was having with her mother, it didn't seem like she was anywhere near ready.

"But my hair," Kaia moaned. "I can't go out looking like this! I'll scare people."

"Just wear your cap for now," her mother replied in a laughing tone. "You can always fix it when you're more awake. Hurry, now, Nolen's waiting."

When they had agreed to go see the nymph's dawn rituals, he hadn't expected it would be so difficult to get her up. Apparently, Kaia wasn't a morning person at all. He'd thought that the way she had been dragging through the days lately was just because she didn't want to be here... After all, she didn't have fond memories of the Silent Marshes.

Now he was seeing things differently.

Finally, she emerged, rubbing her eyes and yawning. She wore a green tunic and black trousers today, but her arms were exposed.

"You should have a sweater on. It's cold in the swamp at this time of the morning," he told her. "And on the way back, you'll be eaten alive."

Kaia frowned but went back into the tent. Soon, however, they were picking their way through a game trail in the swamp. Nolen carried a light stone lantern to guide their way while Kaia stumbled after him, continually yawning.

"Is this really necessary?" she finally asked.

Nolen's enthusiasm had been dampening, and now his heart dropped. "The nymph's dawn ritual is beautiful, and we can't see it any other time. It's one of my favorite things to watch."

"Oh. All right. Sorry for complaining," Kaia picked up her pace and sipped from her waterskin. "I just don't like mornings. I like to stay up late and sleep in late, especially in the summer—It makes the day less hot."

"I love the dawn," Nolen replied. "It's when everything is waking up; it's almost like watching the world come to life. Like these," he added as he spotted some nymph mushrooms. He bent near the small amethyst caps and gently stroked them. "See how closed up and dead they look?"

Kaia crouched near him and nodded.

"These are nymph mushrooms, and they're all connected by one giant mycelium mass throughout the swamp. As soon as the dawn touches one end, it travels throughout the rest of them, and they all open. Watch..." He kept his eyes on the cluster, eager.

Moments later, the caps opened. They spread out like umbrellas, and the thin stalks twisted so that each individual mushroom stood a little apart from the others.

Kaia gasped.

"That's the sign the dawn is coming. Hurry! We don't want to miss the nymphs."

Nolen seized her hand and hurried forward.

Kaia yawned a few times again after that but didn't show she wanted to go back. When they finally got to the nymph rosebushes where Nolen had previously planned, the nymphs were already buzzing about. Nolen's heart jerked, but it didn't seem like they had started their ritual yet.

"Sit down here," Nolen said, brushing some leaves off the log he'd placed here yesterday.

Kaia settled down, and when he sat next to her, she looped her arm through his and moved closer. Her hand was freezing, so he twined his fingers through hers.

"We need to stay quiet," he murmured in her ear.

She shivered, and he frowned.

"Are you cold?"

Kaia shook her head, biting her lip.

"You're shivering."

"I'm fine," Kaia said in a choked sort of voice.

Nolen frowned at her as he shrugged off his jacket and put it around both of their shoulders. "I don't know why you're saying you're not cold when you are. How am I supposed to look out for you if you just lie to me about what you need?"

Kaia peered up at him beneath her lashes.

His heart thumped hard against his ribs as the air left his lungs. Quickly, he turned his face back toward the nymphs. They were flittering about, small balls of light that concealed the tiny humanoid creatures with butterfly wings. These lights were all a dim blue at this point.

The nymphs gathered in a circle, and, as if on cue, music began. Notes from flutes and harps filled the air, with a soft drumbeat in the back. The nymphs sang with it, swaying back and forth as the dark marsh lightened.

Their tiny feet tapped out a complex rhythm on the soft earth as they danced. First circling one way, then the other, then with bursts of flight as they flowed up through the air like a fountain of water. As the sun rose higher and its light grew stronger, the nymphs changed color. Instead of dim blue, they became fiery orange, deep purple, and vibrant green.

They danced with wild abandon as the surrounding foliage grew greener and stood straighter. The circle they danced on bloomed with tiny amethyst mushrooms. They twirled and spun, leaping into other air and fluttering here and there as their wings beat the air.

As the heat of the sun permeated the swamp's coverage, the music grew softer. The nymphs dispersed, their movements growing more languid. Soon, it was only a handful left, and the music faded to nothing as they fluttered away.

And with that, it was over.

Kaia leaned her chin on his shoulder. "That was beautiful. Thank you."

"Thank you for coming. It's one of my favorite things in the world."

"I get why you like to wake up early now," Kaia said. Her warm breath tickled his cheek.

Nolen didn't want to leave the peace of the forest, didn't want to break this connection that he and Kaia were sharing at this moment. "I first saw it as a little boy. There was a grass fire, and as the adults were putting it out, I ran into the forest... I was afraid of fire."

He paused, waiting to see if she would scorn him for that. Kaia only nodded her understanding, her beautiful eyes locked on him.

"I got lost. I'm not sure how far I wandered, but with the silence of the marshes, I couldn't find my way out. A group of nymphs found me and took pity on me. They kept me with them overnight, keeping me warm. In the morning, I saw their ritual. It was the most wonderful thing I had ever seen. After that, I would often come into the marsh looking for them."

"So that's how come they're so friendly with you and don't play pranks," Kaia murmured.

Nolen smiled. "Oh, they still play pranks. I just usually can see them before they strike."

He stroked her hair from her face, smiling at her. She let out a ragged breath and leaned into his hand.

"And?" she pressed.

"And that's pretty well it. I love seeing the morning rituals. It makes me feel alive. No matter how often I see it, I want to see it again and again. Sometimes I'm too busy to get into the swamp at dawn, but—"

Kaia moved forward suddenly, lifting her face to his. Her eyes closed.

Nolen jerked back instinctively.

Both froze. Kaia's eyes flew open again. They stared at each other, and a blush rose on Kaia's cheeks. She pulled back, stiff, as her head ducked.

Oh, no. What was he supposed to say now? Part of Nolen thought he needed to cup her face and kiss her, but his body felt too heavy to move. She had been going to kiss him. That was clear as day. His heart hammered as he sat there, unmoving.

"Sorry," Kaia whispered.

"I'm just not ready for that yet."

Kaia glanced up at him, looking a little miserable. "Not ready for a kiss?"

Nolen blew out his breath and got to his feet. He didn't really want to put more distance between him and Kaia, but it felt too awkward to just sit there like that. He ran a hand through his strawberry-blonde hair.

"No," he said. "I'm not ready for a kiss. Because it's not just a kiss, is it? It's a promise, and I'm just not sure what sort of promise it is. I'm sorry."

"No, I am." Kaia got to her feet as well and took off his jacket, holding it back to him. "The last couple of years, I've been intensely uncomfortable with the sort of attention I've been getting in the romantic sense. If anybody had tried to kiss me, I would have been horrified. I wasn't thinking, and I shouldn't have done that."

Nolen reached for her hand. "Not yet. But we will get there."

Kaia chewed her lip, still not looking at him. "I think we will. We've got a lot of work to do, though."

"I agree with you, there," Nolen said with a laugh. He led her back through the swamp. "But, as I said, we will get there, Kaia. We just have to figure this out."

Kaia smiled at her, the blush receding. "And we will, won't we?"

"Yeah. We will."

CHAPTER
NINE

KAIA HUMMED along with the song that the Swamp Watch was singing as they traipsed back and forth from the pile of brush that had been cleared from the Marshes. Brownies flitted around, sprinkling them with tiny watering cans as thanks for cleaning up the place.

Apparently, this year was a high risk of swamp fires, which risked the peat bogs and methane traps to catch fire. These could be extremely deadly. The brownies were the ones who told the Watch where cleanup needed to happen most, and then the dragons, witches, and humans tended to those areas. Clearing out all this dead, dry stuff would reduce the risk of fire.

"And the baby's in the cradle with the wooden loon, kitty-cat claws at the morning moon," she sang along. Those weren't the right words—not at all—but she didn't actually know the words.

"You're in a good mood today," Mama said, joining her. She and Papa were carrying a heavy log between them.

Kaia grinned. She really was... because she had figured it out. Well, maybe not everything, but the most important thing, at least.

She had spent the early part of the summer feeling like Nolen didn't care what she wanted. That the things which were important to her were things that he just tossed aside without a care, but this morning, when they saw the nymphs, she realized the difference.

Nolen told her that this was important to him. He shared why... she had just assumed that he'd understand the things that were important to her without taking a second thought to tell him why!

He saw the world on different terms. He showed affection differently than she did, and she couldn't just continue to assume things for him.

It wasn't fair to Nolen, and it wasn't fair to her, either.

She dumped her armload of wood into a wagon. Some of it would be processed into lumber, others into pulp for paper, but the vast majority of it would be mulched and composted to be returned into the swamp so that the ground didn't lose the nutrients that it otherwise would get.

Taking a moment to drink from her waterskin, she turned to watch Nolen and a handful of the other Watch members as they worked. Nolen was laughing as he hauled massive blocks of wood. Everything about him was at ease and relaxed, his silver eyes sparkling with delight.

He was so handsome.

He never shied back from hard work but was incredibly in tune with those around him. He kind of reminded her of Wickham in that way, how he would catch when other people needed to take a rest.

"Admiring your mate?" Mama teased.

"He's such a hard worker," Kaia replied. "I never thought about it, but he did so much work at the schloss. Fixed the dock, took out all those burr bushes I was ruining my skirts on, built a walkway from the schloss to the lake... he was always busy."

She had thought he was avoiding her by finding things to do at the time. Now, though, she realized he liked to keep busy, and she should have taken the time to hang out with him. They could have worked together or even just talked while he worked.

He was noticing what she needed and improving her life. It made her heart ache as she realized just how selfish she had been not to see it before.

Papa chuckled as he kissed the top of her head, then he and Mama went back to work.

Nolen and the others chopped up the larger pieces of log now, and they formed a chain to pass them from one to the other and toss them into another wagon.

"Always work to be done," she murmured as she headed over to join the chain; her legs ached, and she hoped that being in one place and just twisting back and forth would be a little easier.

They started up a new song; one Kaia hadn't heard before. It reminded her of the old sea shanties her grandfather used to sing as lullabies. The work was hard—she was shocked at how much physical labor there was involved in the Watch—but it was a rewarding difficulty.

Kaia was never one who enjoyed hard work. She didn't think that she would continue to find this rewarding if she had to do it all year long, but that was the beauty of the Watch. With so much work to be done, you could always go do something else. Cooking, cleaning, patching clothes, setting up the tents, keeping an eye out for wildlife, hiking the swamp for any dangerous spots, guiding tourists... there were so many distinct possibilities.

Once the log chain was done, Kaia headed to the water station. She rolled her sore shoulders as she found a seat and drank deeply.

Nolen joined her, sprawling on the ground next to her. "I hope this hasn't ruined your pretty clothes," he said, a crease between his brows. "You really should wear some older clothes when we're doing this sort of thing—it's difficult to get the sap out of fabric."

Kaia shook her head with a small laugh. "I don't think you realize that these are my old clothes. Everything I own is pretty. I *love* pretty clothes."

"They aren't very practical."

"I disagree." Kaia held her arms out. "This is good, sturdy fabric. It cleans easily and dries quickly. It's not so old as to be threadbare and doesn't tear easily. The sleeves are loose enough to roll up if I need to. Very practical."

Nolen pinched one frill on her shoulder. "And this?"

Kaia cocked her head. "Does it get in the way? Does it make it more difficult to do my work?"

"No," Nolen said slowly. "I suppose not."

"Then it's not impractical at all. I know it might be strange since you keep everything to a minimum—you have to," she added quickly, so he would know she wasn't criticizing him, "because you're always on the move, you don't have the space to have unnecessary things. But I like to add bows and ribbons where I can."

"I suppose I can understand that," Nolen said with a slight nod. "Small things that make you happy and don't get in the way?"

"Exactly. It's not like I'm wearing a ballgown... although I would if I could get away with it," Kaia said with a laugh. "I just love feeling beautiful."

"You're always beautiful, though."

Kaia blushed and smiled. She loved it when he said things like that. "Thank you."

Nolen frowned. "Why are you saying thank you? It's true?"

"It's still a compliment, and I can still say thank you."

It was Nolen's turn to blush. He flipped to lie on his stomach and picked at the grass. "Er, you're welcome. That's one of those rude things, isn't it?"

"Yes. I know you don't mean it to be rude, but it is a little rude," Kaia relented. Even though she wanted to reassure him, she also didn't want to just say everything was all right when it wasn't... she didn't mind in this case, but there would be times when it upset her to be spoken to like that.

Nolen let out a heavy breath. "Sorry. Sometimes I forget I'm not talking to Odele. She's always so literal. Usually, I'm the one having to explain things to her... I'm not used to being out of my depth, socially."

Kaia nodded her understanding. "And I shoved way too much at out all at once. Now that we're here, I can understand how my family was too much... I just wanted them all to love you. They're important to me, and even though there's a bajillion of them, I love them all."

Nolen stared at the blade of grass he shredded with his thumbnail.

"Actually, I wanted to talk to you about that first day when we went into town," Kaia said slowly.

"I don't—"

"Please?"

Nolen huffed. "I don't see why. It's over and done with."

"But you don't know that it's traditional for everyone in the family to heap more presents on a recent addition than what they know how to do with," Kaia said gently. "That's what I wanted to say."

"They do that to everyone?" Nolen finally looked up, his silver eyes wide. "They didn't just think I looked... wrong?"

"Not at all. Looking back, I can see that you were uncomfortable with everything that was offered to you. At the time, I thought you were rejecting my family, not their gifts. But physical things like that aren't important to you... they'd actively make your life harder," she added because it was true. He had to keep his possessions slimmed down for as often as the Watch moved around.

Nolen rolled to a sitting position. "I thought that they just didn't like my clothes."

Kaia shook her head. "Not at all. And because you kept refusing everything, I thought you were just being stubborn and prideful. I was wrong... and I'm sorry for making assumptions.

"I thought they were all judging me," Nolen murmured. "I'm sorry for making my own assumptions."

He held out his hand, and Kaia took it. They smiled at each other, and one more weight lifted off Kaia's shoulders.

Communication, just like Mama said. *That's what makes mates stick together.*

CHAPTER

TEN

THE AIR WAS HOT, and sweat was making Nolen's clothes cling to him by the time they called it quits for the day. Even though there was plenty more work to be done, they had gotten a lot completed already, and it was time to take a well-deserved break. Nolen took Kaia to the large, sluggish river that bordered the Silent Marshes on this side.

The two of them hiked upriver a couple of miles, then waded into the cool water to float back down.

"It's only a month before we have to go back to school," Nolen said.

Kaia wrinkled her nose. "Don't remind me! We'll be going to Thunder Ridge this year. I love rocs, I think they're beautiful birds, but they scare me. I don't see why we have to go there, of all places."

"Because the mountain range is imbued with magic that's useful for us dragons," Nolen told her, though he wasn't entirely certain if she was being serious or not.

Kaia laughed and splashed him. "Oh, I know that. I'm just complaining for no reason."

Nolen rolled his eyes. "Oh, I see. But roc attacks are extremely rare. We'll be fine."

"Given our year's track record?" Kaia's cheerful expression darkened. "If anyone was going to be attacked, it would be us."

Nolen flinched. Of course. Their year had seen an unusual number of difficulties. Nobody else could say that they dealt with being kidnapped three years in a row... although technically, this last year's kidnapping wasn't in the same level of danger as the first two, it was still becoming a pattern.

Kaia dove under the water and kicked against the current, bringing herself up several meters upriver. Nolen found a large rock to brace himself against and stood, waiting for her to come back.

"You're more comfortable with my parents now," she said when they were close together again. She dipped her face under water so just her eyes were sticking out.

The sudden change of topic disoriented him for a moment, but Nolen nodded. "Yeah. They're fun to be around. I'm glad they're starting to like me and aren't holding all my mess-ups against me."

He held out his arms and caught Kaia as she floated past. Though the river wasn't fast, his feet were pulled from their tenuous grasp, and they went bobbing along, holding onto each other's arms as they kicked their feet and spun in lazy circles.

"What do you mean they aren't holding your mess-ups against you? What mess-ups?"

Nolen opened his mouth to answer, but they hit an eddie at that moment, and he was slapped in the face with a wave. He choked on it and had to release Kaia as he hacked and coughed, which only pulled him under the water and made him risk breathing in more.

Kaia tugged on his arm, and they made their way to the shore, where Nolen finally got his breath back. He stood straight, taking deep breaths through his nose.

"Are you okay?" Kaia asked worriedly.

Nolen nodded.

"If you didn't want to answer, you could have just said so," she teased gently, though her brow was still furrowed with concern.

Nolen took a deep breath, in part to test his lungs but also to give himself another few seconds to think. "I mean, like when I used the wrong fork, or I was dancing the foxtrot instead of the waltz... and, of course, when I blew up at you."

Kaia wiped her wet silver hair from her eyes. "But... none of that mattered. I mean, blowing up, sure, but you apologized, and that's all that matters with that. But nobody cared about the fork or the dancing."

"Then why were you always correcting me?" Nolen blurted before he could think better of it.

Kaia's chin dropped. Nolen started to say it didn't matter, but she held up a hand toward him, showing she wanted time to think. Nolen crouched back into the cool, clear water as he waited.

What was she thinking?

"That's my fault," she finally said. "I knew it wasn't a big deal, but I made it into a big deal by bringing it up. Nobody cared... and yet, I cared for some reason. I think maybe I just didn't like the reminders that we are really from two different walks of life. I thought if we're meant to be perfect for each other, that meant the same."

"Oh." He wasn't sure what else to say.

"I'm sorry. I shouldn't have made such a big deal over those little things, and I should have been more open with my communication."

Nolen had to chuckle a little at that. "I should have, too. I should have explained to your family that the Watch moves around often, so I didn't have the space for their gifts. I didn't."

"Seems to me like maybe we both messed up, just a little," Kaia said, pinching her finger and thumb close together. "Are you okay with getting back into the water?"

Nolen nodded.

They waded back into the middle of the river and resumed their floating. This was exactly what he had wanted from the start of the summer, a time when they could just be together and talk like this. Just look at how well it was going now?

But there was still a cloud hanging over them, despite their clearing the air. "You still want me to get to know your family. You're going to want to have major celebrations with them and have times when they're all swarming around the schloss."

Kaia nodded. "I love it when we're all together. It's exhausting even for me, but it makes me feel so loved to have them all there."

"I'm not sure if I can adapt to that," Nolen confessed, wincing as he did so. "That much noise and that many people without a space to go and just have absolute silence... it's a nightmare for me. I don't know if I could enjoy it, even for a few days."

Kaia blew out a breath underwater so that bubbles popped into her face.

Nolen stretched out to float on his back, letting his hands trail behind him. He understood that Kaia's family was a major part of her life, and he needed to figure out how to be okay with that. He needed to spend time with them without blowing up...

"I'm going to have to apologize to all of them," he muttered, his voice muffled by the water in his ears. "I yelled at you in front of them; I need to apologize to you in front of them and to all of them, too. But I can't wait until we're all gathered together; I should have apologized already. I'll have to write—"

He stopped as Kaia pulled on his foot.

Nolen straightened himself, leaving his isolated little world.

"Thank you for thinking about that. I really appreciate that you're considering what you have to do." She bobbed in the water.

"Right now, though, can we focus on figuring out how to make it work for you to get to know my family, so you can be more comfortable with them."

Nolen sighed. "Are any of your cousins at the Institute?"

Kaia shook her head. "Not yet. I was the last of the first generation of cousins, and the younger ones—my cousins' kids, aren't old enough to go to the Silver Springs."

So that left out meeting them on neutral ground. Nolen considered it further, then shook his head. "All I can really think right now is that it'll be best to introduce them a few at a time, so I can get to know them better in a smaller setting rather than so many all at once."

"I think we can make that work," Kaia agreed.

She grinned at him, and his heart fluttered. Part of him wanted to kiss her... but he pulled himself back. Like he told her before, there was a promise in the first kiss that he wasn't ready to make yet.

He wasn't sure if the idea of introducing her family to him slowly would make enough of a difference. After all, she would still want the massive get-togethers. They were important to her.

But it was the first step to take to make it work. For now, it would be enough.

CHAPTER
ELEVEN

THEY RETURNED to the camp to find everyone in a flurry. It seemed the same as every other day to Kaia, but Nolen abruptly went quiet. His gaze grew serious as he grabbed her hand and quickly found his parents.

"A human hiker has gone missing in the marsh," his mother said as she handed Nolen a backpack. "We have a grid pattern for the search. Kaia, will you be all right going with him?"

Kaia nodded, though she felt bewildered. "I'm not sure how much good I'll do."

His mother gave her a tight smile. "Only witches can hear the sounds that travel in the marshes. To Nolen, it'll be silent. But you might hear calls for help."

Oh. Right! Kaia winced—she shouldn't have forgotten that. She was given a pack as well, which she pulled onto her shoulders and buckled around her waist. Luckily, she and Nolen had dried out in the sun before heading back. They didn't need to change before heading into the swamp.

"The hiker was last seen near Maggie's nest," Nolen's mother continued.

Kaia's brows knit. "Maggie?"

Nolen fixed one strap on her pack. "A kelpie that likes to follow us around and cause trouble."

A kelpie? Kaia swallowed hard. She didn't think kelpies were this close to the edge of the swamp. She didn't have any experience with them herself, but Penelope had nearly drowned their first year.

"It's all right if you want to stay in the camp," Nolen said, catching the look on her face. "I know the swamp; I can do my part on my own."

Kaia shook her head. "No. No, I'll go with you. I'm supposed to help others, too. I'm a witch. And I'm supposed to help you."

She gave him a fierce, determined look. Nolen smiled at her with soft eyes. He didn't look worried at all, and that helped her to feel better. Maybe hikers getting lost was common enough that he had every confidence that they'd find the missing human soon enough.

"Are you sure?" Nolen asked her. His brows pinched.

Kaia threw her shoulders back. "Yes. I spent quite a few weeks in the Marshes, remember? Trying to find someone who is lost has got to be much more enjoyable than running away from Odentia warriors."

Nolen smirked at her. "Let's get going, then. I know where we can find a brownie nest to get them to help... but we might have to cut off some of your hair," he warned as he led toward the swamp. "They love shiny, soft things, and your hair is beautiful."

Even though it was greasy and tangled up in knots? She had all but given up on trying to brush it, instead keeping it in tight braids pinned to her head so that they wouldn't get even worse. Already she thought she was going to have to cut off the split ends and a good deal of the tangles to be presentable for the Institute again...

But she still glowed from Nolen's casual praise.

Soon, they were in the swamp. It was cool and quiet this time of day. Kaia pulled out the wand that Nolen had given her the previous year and pointed it at their feet. She rubbed her thumb against the smooth wood, weighing her words.

Intent mattered more than words with this sort of spell, but it also took a great deal of energy. She might put herself in a coma if she tried to just order the magic to show them where to go. If it was that easy, the adults would already do it.

"I think maybe it's best if we save the magic," Nolen suggested, glancing at her. "Until we have a better idea of where they went. Come on, Maggie's nest is this way."

Kaia stowed her wand back in the pouch at her waist. "Shouldn't we avoid the kelpie?"

"Maggie's grumpy, but she's pretty harmless as it goes," Nolen told her, holding his hand out reassuringly. "Trust me. I'll look after you."

Kaia accepted his hand. It felt like they wandered through the game trails for hours, but Nolen seemed to know exactly where they were going. They came to a fast-flowing river, over which was... well, it wasn't a bridge. It was three ropes, one strung tightly along the top and the other two at a level to hold on to.

Kaia's heart leaped to her throat, and she stopped dead. "I can't go across that! I'll fall."

Nolen grasped the two top ropes. "I go across it all the time."

"But I don't! I'll fall."

Nolen blew out a breath; then his face lit up. "Use magic. Give your feet a good grip on the rope."

Kaia whipped out her wand, excited. She pointed it at her feet. "Stay true and steadfast, and don't let me slip off the rope."

A beam of light shot from the tip of the wand to wrap around her feet. The light lingered as Kaia put her wand away.

Nolen stepped to one side, letting Kaia go first. Her heart pounded as she took the first step. To her delight, the little rope seemed as wide beneath her foot as a plank of wood. With more confidence, she strode forward.

"Wait," Nolen called suddenly—

The rope snapped.

Kaia tumbled down, instantly submerged in the river. White foam surrounded her. A hand grabbed her arm and yanked her upward; then she felt Nolen's firm grasp on her hips as he pushed her toward the surface. Her head broke, and she gasped noisily, trying to pull Nolen up as well. As he came closer to the surface, she went under again.

Rushing water filled her ears and streamed into her nose and mouth. She couldn't see anything. Her lungs were screaming for air by the time her feet hit a rock. They stuck. Nolen was nearly ripped away from her, but she clung to him. Step by step, Kaia dragged herself close enough to shore for Nolen to get a foothold, too.

They pulled themselves onto the shore and collapsed into the moss, coughing until their lungs were raw.

Before Kaia felt like she could even move, though, Nolen was on his feet. He raced down beside the river; Kaia tried to call after him, only to end up in another coughing fit. Where was he going? Had he seen a threat? Why was he leaving her?

She had just pulled herself into a sitting position when Nolen returned. Water still dripped from him, and his breathing was hoarse as he dragged a pack behind him.

Kaia blinked, then glanced around. Neither of their packs were anywhere around... Vaguely, she remembered Nolen's hands moving over her under the water, unfastening the pack. The weight of it being lifted off her before he heaved her out of the water for a precious gasp of air.

"Couldn't find the other one," Nolen grunted, tossing the pack down. "We'll set camp. Get a fire going, and dry out. Yeah."

Kaia checked her pouch. Her precious wand was still there, and she sighed in relief. Her chest ached from the coughing, but she still had her wand.

"I'll start drying things out," she said, pulling the pack toward her.

"Save your energy," Nolen replied.

Kaia flinched at his harsh tone. He must blame her for what happened... she knew she was bigger than a lot of girls her age, but she never thought that she'd break a rope like that. She chewed her lip, trying desperately not to cry.

Instead, she reached for the wood.

Nolen walked over to her and took her hands in his. "I said save your energy. You swallowed a lot of water. I'd rather you rest and recover rather than push yourself too hard."

"I can help."

"Kaia—"

"Nolen," she snapped back, narrowing her eyes.

Tension pulsed in the air between them.

Nolen released her hands and stepped back. "Why are you angry with me?"

"Because you're angry with me! It's not my fault the rope broke."

"I know that! I'm not angry at you—I'm angry at myself!" Nolen clenched his fists at his sides, panting. His jaw was locked at the same time as their gazes. "I know I messed up. So just try to get some rest while I figure out how to fix it."

CHAPTER
TWELVE

NOLEN BREATHED HARD, bracing himself. He admitted it. He messed up. They were only in this situation because of him. Kaia had nearly drowned because of him. It was his job to ensure everything was safe before proceeding. He knew that the creatures of the marshes would mess with the bridges that they left; he knew he needed to check them for any wear before letting Kaia go across.

Instead, he's only seen how much it was frayed at the other side of the river after Kaia had stepped out onto it. By then, it was too late.

It was their first summer together, and he had almost killed his fated mate already.

"What...?" Kaia's angry expression melted away. Her tense shoulders dropped as she pushed her wet hair from her face. "What are you talking about? The rope broke because I was too heavy."

Nolen shook his head. Even though he was the one who had messed up, she was still blaming herself! "It was frayed. I should have seen it. I should have—"

"Nolen." Kaia stepped forward.

He waited for her to continue, searching her gaze. The lack of reproach in her eyes made him feel worse, somehow. She should be angry with him, and yet she was looking at him with so much compassion... he didn't know what to do with that.

"Blaming yourself won't help. This is one of those situations where what's done is done. We just have to move forward, having learned from our mistakes." She gave him a smile, and though it was small, it seemed genuine. "For right now, let's concentrate on what we need to do. You said we needed a fire, right?"

Nolen nodded.

"Then let's get wood for a fire."

He hesitated but nodded. Kaia seemed to be healthy enough now, and her breathing was clear. Maybe she wasn't in as bad of shape as he had feared.

They started working together, and soon not only had the fire going but also sorted through the pack. Most of the contents had survived, perfectly usable if wet. Nolen set up the canvas to shelter them from any potential storms, and they settled down to cook some of their preserves.

"I'm sorry I caused you so much stress," Kaia said as she stirred some fresh twigs into the fire.

Shock rippled through Nolen.

"If I paid better attention to all our wilderness survival training, maybe you wouldn't feel you need to talk care of me."

"But you don't cause me stress. You've handled yourself wonderfully."

Kaia dropped her stick beside herself and glared at him, but tears glimmered in her eyes. "You're just trying to make me feel better. I'm always causing you to stress. It's my fault that rope broke, no matter what you say. I'm the one who went out there and wasn't holding on to the support ropes. So, I'm the one who lost our packs. Not to mention foisting my family on you without regarding whether you were ready or not."

Nolen's expression softened. He turned her to him and took both of her hands in his. "It's not your fault. I know that we're in a tough situation, but that doesn't mean I think you're helpless."

"You kept pushing me above the surface of the river, even if it meant going under yourself."

Nolen couldn't help but smirk at her, shaking his head. "Only because you were doing the same thing."

"I was?"

"You were." His smile faded. "And you shouldn't have. I'm the dragon shifter. It's my job to protect you, Kaia. You shouldn't feel you have to protect me."

To his surprise, Kaia scoffed. "You can't really think that, can you? Not after you just got through saying I'm not helpless."

"It's my job to protect you; that doesn't make you helpless."

"Your job is to be my partner, just like I'm meant to be your partner." Kaia stirred the food.

Nolen watched her, admiring how quickly she could put her frustrations behind her. Even now, she was speaking as though what she said was factual but without judgment, even though he knew she must still be shaken by everything.

He took a deep breath. "I didn't think I'd be a dragon. I thought I'd be human. I didn't want to be a dragon. And now that I am... I don't know what I'm supposed to do. I feel so overwhelmed all the time, and now that we're mates...."

He bowed his head, ashamed.

"Now that we're mates?" Kaia pressed. Her voice shook.

"You've already been through so much. All that stuff with Finnegan, the Sprites... I'm just... I don't know if I'm enough to protect you. What if my desire not to be a dragon makes it so I can't shift next year? What if something went wrong, and I'm not actually a dragon? I should be stronger; I should be smarter. I should be able to protect you."

Kaia pulled him into a hug. Her face pressed into his shoulder.

Nolen almost pulled away. Not because he didn't want the hug but because his clothes were still damp. He didn't want to chill her any more than she already was.

Which, he realized, was silly. She was just as damp as he was, and the air was warm with the fire's heat reflected off the tarp back at them.

"Remember what I was saying earlier about not needing to be perfect?" Kaia whispered.

Nolen nodded, hugging her in return.

"You don't have to be perfect to protect me. You don't have to be invincible or make no mistakes. We're supposed to be partners, and partners support each other. Like everything else, we need communication. When the time comes for you to shift into your dragon form, we'll figure out any problems that arise then."

She pulled back and grinned at him.

Nolen pulled his hand through his pale hair, shivering as he imagined everything that could go wrong in the next few years. But when it came down to it, those problems weren't here yet. Kaia was right. They couldn't plan for everything... and as much as he would like to be perfect, he couldn't be.

"Thank you." Nolen took a deep breath. "I know it seems like I have it together most of the time, but that's only because I've learned not to show my emotions. I always try my best to look like I'm cool-headed because all my life, I've needed to be. Panicking never makes a situation better."

"I understand. But we're in this together, okay?"

He smiled back and took the now-bubbling food off the fire. "Yeah. I think I am going to be okay."

"First thing we need to figure out... how to eat this without burning our fingers," Kaia said, staring longingly at the food. "We don't have any cutlery left. Maybe if we use some sticks...."

Nolen scooped out a little of their strew on the stirring spoon and blew on it. "We've got a spoon right here. We'll just have to share."

Kaia started, then laughed. "Oh! I never even thought of that. How silly!"

He offered her the first bite. "Too proper a lady to think about eating off a utensil. Us roughers have to do what we can."

Kaia giggled as she chewed her first bite. "Roughers?"

"I don't know. I was thinking about 'roughing it,' and I couldn't think of any other way to say it."

"Roughers is fine." She winked at him.

Nolen gave himself a hearty spoonful of the food. Now that they were getting warm and had some food to fill their bellies, he was feeling much better. Or maybe that was because he and Kaia had talked. He certainly felt much better about what had happened and their future together.

"I was thinking," Nolen said as Kaia dished herself another spoonful, "when we get back to camp, we should ask about one of your cousin's families joining us. One without little children," he added, grimacing.

"Do you not like children?"

"I like them okay in small doses," Nolen said. "But with the marshes, we'd have to put leashes on them to make sure they didn't wander off. Not every nymph nest is as kind as the one that found me."

Kaia nodded seriously. "Heather and Gregory, I think, then. Just two to begin with, and they're closest to our age."

Nolen let out a relieved breath. That sounded like a good step. "I can deal with that."

"Good. Now, less talking, more eating!" Kaia dug into the stew again with gusto.

Nolen watched her with admiration. She really was the smartest person he'd ever met.

CHAPTER

THIRTEEN

KAIA TURNED her back to the fire. Once they had eaten their fill, they built the fire higher to dry out their clothes better. Night had fallen some time ago, and the Silent Marshes were... well, silent. Not that they were incredibly noisy during the day, but a hush fell over the night that sent shivers down her spine.

"I hope they don't have to come looking for us," Kaia said as she ruffled her fingers through her hair, making sure it had dried all the way through. "I'd hate for that hiker to be missed because too many resources were split up."

"We'll head back to camp first thing in the morning," Nolen told her. He was whipping the sole surviving blanket back and forth in the air, trying to dry it. "Don't worry, though. We all have spells on us so that the camp leader knows how to find us if we go missing."

Kaia turned again and crouched next to the fire. It was a shame that the foliage was so thick around them. If it was thinner, maybe the light would go farther, and the hiker could find them.

Her eyes widened. Of course! She shot to her feet again. "Nolen!

What sort of magic do you have in the Watch for search and rescue?"

Nolen jumped at the urgency in her voice. "Er... mostly healers. The witches get together to put blessings on the camp for its protection, but generally, it's the dragons who do the searching, not the witches."

She thought so. Kaia grinned as she pulled her wand from its pouch. She looked around and found a small bunch of nymph mushrooms. Their umbrella heads had closed for the night, turning into tiny little caps.

"What are you doing?" Nolen asked. He hung the blanket over a tree branch.

Kaia knelt by the mushrooms and pointed her wand at them. "They whom we search for find us instead."

A wave of tiredness washed over her. She swayed on the spot, but even as Nolen jumped forward, it passed. The mushrooms glowed softly; then, the light faded away entirely. Kaia could feel the energy of the forest pulsing around her. She closed her eyes, sensing the magic in the trees just as well as she could hear the river rushing.

"Kaia?" Nolen asked, putting a hand on her shoulder.

She straightened. "I put a spell into the nymph mushrooms so that the lost hiker will find us. I don't know if it will work, but you told me they were all connected. So maybe it will work. It's an idea, at least."

Nolen beamed at her. "That's brilliant!"

"I'm sure Herja would have already come up with it."

"Oh, Herja is too practical for that. I've never heard anything where a witch uses fungi to transport a spell... maybe Wickham and Herja both could have figured it out. But you..." Nolen beamed at her. "You're so smart."

Kaia couldn't remember when she had been called smart before. At least, not like this. It made butterflies erupt in her stomach.

"Thanks. We'll see if it works, though."

She settled down next to the fire again, Nolen next to her. A break in the canopy above them showed that the purple twilight had changed to night. A few of the first stars were appearing overhead.

"The kelpie won't come for us, will it?" Kaia asked as she found a comfortable spot to lie down.

Nolen lay down next to her, both their feet pointed at the fire. "Nah. Maggie especially is afraid of fire, although all kelpies are. The ones we really have to worry about is brownies if they decide we're being too noisy. But I'll be able to talk them down if they show up."

"Good. I don't really like kelpies... they scare me."

Nolen arched a brow at her. "Is this the same girl that tried to rescue a baby griffon on our way to the Silver Springs?"

"It was after, and griffons are cute." Kaia thought a moment and shrugged. "Besides, just because rocs and kelpies scare me doesn't mean I wouldn't try to rescue their babies if I thought they were in danger."

She folded her arms behind her head, staring up at the stars as they grew stronger above them. They were beautiful, all silver and sparkling. As she breathed in the cool summer night air, she thought about that night when they learned they were fated mates. How pleased she was when she found the fine silver threads connecting the two of them together.

"I'm glad you're my fated mate," she told him, comfortable despite the damp chill and the hard ground. "I made sure that I could see how all the dragons would be good matches, but I hoped it would be you. And it is."

"I'm glad you're my mate, too."

Kaia smiled, satisfied.

"Go ahead and get some sleep," Nolan said, already sounding like he was struggling to stay awake. "I'll take first watch."

"No, you sleep. I like to stay up late. You like to get up early. Fair's fair." Kaia pushed herself back up and added a log to the fire. She was determined to let her mate sleep, and it was also true. She was better suited for the late nights, anyway.

Nolen fell asleep quickly. With nobody to talk to, Kaia grew bored, so she got up and walked around the edge of their camp, listening to the sounds of the marsh at night.

Just when she was thinking she needed to wake Nolen and have him take over watch, she heard bushes rustling as though something heavy was moving through them. She tensed up, her heart jumping to her throat as she realized something was coming through them.

She rushed to Nolen's side and shook him awake. His eyes snapped open, and he rolled up, seemingly fully alert.

"Something's coming," Kaia hissed.

"Get ready to run," Nolen murmured back. He pulled a knife from his belt.

Then a thin, frightened voice called from somewhere beyond the trees. "Hello?"

"Oh!" Kaia jumped back to her feet. "It's them—it's the hiker."

Nolen kept the knife out as he squinted into the darkness. "Where?"

She pointed.

"Stay here," he said, then headed into the bushes.

Kaia stayed near the fire and listened to the sounds of bushes moving. Soon, voices joined that noise. First, a surprised shout, followed by Nolen's soothing tones. Then sobbing.

Moments later, Nolen came back, leading the missing human with him. It was a young man with a giant bruise forming on his forehead. Kaia immediately took care of his injury, trying to remember the times she helped Wickham in these situations.

"I kept seeing fires flickering in the distance, but when I got closer, they were only mushrooms," the boy said, tears streaking down his face. "I thought I was going crazy."

"You aren't crazy," Nolen assured him. "My mate cast a spell to help you find your way back out. And it worked." He grinned up at her, and the pride in his eyes took her breath away.

It had really worked.

CHAPTER
FOURTEEN

AFTER KAIA and Nolen rescued the human boy from the swamp, there was a celebration at the Watch. The two new mates shared a night of music and food. Nolen and Kaia kept dancing until their feet were sore. It was that night that Kaia finally told Nolen how much she enjoyed walking beneath the stars, and they agreed to swap between the nighttime walks and early mornings for the nymph's rituals once every week.

The next day, Kaia's parents told her they had decided it was time for them to take their leave, as the original agreement was for Kaia to be with the Watch without them.

Ironically, it was Nolen who was initially hesitant about them leaving. He didn't want her to end up overwhelmed and feeling isolated like he had. But Kaia assured him that she was fine, and her parents took off.

After that, the rest of the summer went smoothly. Heather and Gregory did come for a visit and stayed for a couple of weeks before leaving again. More of Kaia's extended family slowly cycled through, but only a few at the time. Even so, Nolen did find it overwhelming—but here on familiar ground, it was much better than it had been.

"I only wish we had done it this way from the start," Kaia told him one evening during their nighttime stroll.

"Better figuring it out late than never, though, right?" Nolen replied.

Kaia laughed and slipped her hand into his. "I'm glad that you're more comfortable with me. I know I was putting a lot of pressure on our relationship, but I was getting worried that nothing was going to go as I thought it would."

"I know what you mean."

Nolen smiled to himself. The summer had been spent working together, figuring out what each other's needs in this partnership was. He was surprised at just how much talking there was involved in it. He didn't have to talk to his family much; they had worked together in such tight quarters for so long that it was like they could read each other's minds.

He had a lot to learn, but luckily, he did like learning... so long as there was no studying involved!

"I have something I want to ask you," he said a little hesitantly.

"Mmm?"

Nolen took a deep breath. "When we get back to the Institute... do you want to start dating?"

Kaia looked at their hands. "Isn't this dating?"

"Er... I guess, but it's not deliberate dating. I mean, like dinners and dressing up and all that." Nolen's cheeks burned. "Fancy things."

"I'd love that."

"Good. Good!" Nolen laughed with giddiness. He already had so many ideas!

"But," Kaia said, pulling him to a stop, "every time we go on a date, we have to make it clear that it's a date. I'd hate for you to take me out somewhere you're excited for, only for me not to realize it's a date and to do something wrong."

"For sure." Nolen nodded.

The two of them had talked deeply about their different communication styles and had promised to work on learning how to talk to each other better. The most important thing they'd both agreed on was that they couldn't assume anything about what the other was thinking.

It was better to over-communicate than not communicate at all, they decided. It certainly didn't work like in the stories where young fated mates automatically knew what each other were thinking.

They continued their walk, the stars twinkling overhead.

After that conversation, Nolen spent many hours planning the dates he would take Kaia on. He knew he wanted them to have reasons for her to dress up since she loved it so much, but he wasn't entirely certain how to get there. He talked to his parents and others in the Watch and came up with a bunch of different ideas he was excited to try out.

Odele didn't return to the Watch at all over the summer. Kaia went back home for the last week, and Nolen anxiously counted the days, filled with hard work as they were.

When his father flew him to the Institute, he could hardly wait to get started on the school year. Odele and Adina were already there, although Kaia was going to be later—she had her farewell celebration with her family to have yet. Nolen had written personal apologies to each one, and they had all expressed happiness at his apology.

He had a feeling the next time he met them—or at least, the next batch—things were going to be much, much better.

"I missed you," Nolen told Odele as he hugged her.

"Not too much, I hope," Odele replied.

"Oh, I kept busy. But I'm always going to miss my little sister."

Odele punched his arm. "Twin sister, you mean."

"I was born first." Nolen grinned at her. "So, how was your summer at the palace?"

Odele tapped her chin as she thought. "Dramatic," she finally said.

Adina laughed. "It certainly was! Your sister nearly got herself married to not one but all nine princes from Weastrom."

"I did not!"

Finally, it was the night of the welcoming feast, and when Nolen, Odele, and Adina went to the feast, he was thrilled to find Kaia there, sitting with Wickham, Herja, and Penelope. Nolen rushed over and swept her into his arms, laughing as she squealed in excitement.

"Sit with me," she said as she pulled a chair between hers and Wickham's. "I have so much to tell you!"

"I do, too," Nolen said seriously. "I'm a prince now."'

Kaia's eyes widened.

"He is not!" Odele shouted from where she and Adina had set with Xena, Vera, Jalene, and Icarus. "That wedding never happened. And even if it did, I'd be a princess. He wouldn't be a prince."

Kaia looked even more surprised, and Nolen had to laugh. "It's quite a story. I'll tell you later."

Headmaster Valiant stood in front of the group, lifting his arms to call for quiet. Kaia leaned in closer to Nolen.

"You'd better tell me. That's too juicy to drop on me and leave me hanging."

"After the food, let's go for a walk," Nolen suggested. Days got darker at the Institute than at the Silent Marshes, at least during this time of year. "The stars have been gorgeous lately."

Kaia's eyes lit up, sparkling just like the stars.

The feast took longer than he expected, but he still loved it. The noise and people didn't bother him as much as they normally would. Maybe because every time he got overwhelmed, Kaia would put a dampening spell on his ears so that the worst of the noise was blocked out.

Afterward, they took a walk, catching each other up on everything in the past week—there was a surprising amount to talk about.

When they came to a stop next to the pond, Kaia turned to Nolen. "So, I had a thought about our star threads. I'd like to weave them into a blanket. One that we can take with us when we're camping or when we go on picnics. And I can keep it sometimes, and you can keep it sometimes."

"I love that idea. And when we have a fight, we pull it out, and we come out here to sit under the stars with our blanket and talk things out," Nolen suggested.

Kaia beamed. She chewed her lip as she gazed into his eyes. The nerves were plain on her face, but there was excitement, too. "I'm going to ask you something. And if you say no, I won't bring it up again."

A burst of nerves went through his gut. "Yes?"

"May I kiss you?"

A fuzzy warm feeling spread across Nolen's chest. He grinned as he stepped forward. "Yes."

He lowered his head toward hers as she tilted up her face. And under the twinkling lights of the stars, they shared their first kiss.

The End

Read *The Quest for the Phantom Feather*, the third book in the *Defenders of the Realm* series!

If you enjoyed this book, please consider leaving a review on
Amazon, Goodreads, or <u>Bookbub.</u>
Reviews help me reach new readers.

Join my newsletter at www.mhlebeault.com for writing
updates, sneak peaks, review copies, sales, and giveaways!

www.ingramcontent.com/pod-product-compliance
Lightning Source LLC
Chambersburg PA
CBHW021129130626
46554CB00002B/923

something more tangible: guidance.

Section Four is where this book shifts into a practical toolkit. Here you'll find questions to bring to your doctor, strategies for handling side effects, ways to manage the emotional toll, and insights for both patients and caregivers. If the earlier sections were about perspective, this one is about tools you can use right now. And if you'd like printable versions of the checklists and questions, you can download them at any time from:

vikkiespinosawrites.com/pages/resources

SECTION FOUR

A Guide for Patients and Caregivers

Cancer is overwhelming, and so is the amount of information thrown at you. This section gathers the questions, tips, and coping tools I wish I'd had when I was in the thick of it. Think of it as a resource you can turn to whenever you need clarity.

Chapter 19: Breast Cancer Diagnosis: It's Complicated

When I was first diagnosed, I had no idea how many different kinds of breast cancer there were. I thought breast cancer was just...breast cancer. Either you had it, or you didn't. I didn't know that some women are diagnosed with DCIS—ductal carcinoma in situ—often called "stage 0." It hasn't spread outside the milk ducts. While it still requires treatment, it's different from invasive cancers that move into surrounding tissue.

I also didn't know how much weight doctors place on lymph nodes. Whether or not cancer cells are found in the lymph nodes changes staging, treatment, and prognosis. A tumor that looks small and manageable can become much more serious once lymph nodes are involved.

What I've since learned is that "breast cancer" is an umbrella term. Underneath it are countless variations, each with its own treatment path. Which is why comparing one woman's journey to another's doesn't work.

Breast Cancer by the Numbers: It's More Common than You Think

Breast cancer is **the** most common cancer among women. While we often associate it with older adults, it is now being diagnosed more frequently in younger women.

- **Approximately 1 in 8 women** in the United States (about 13%) will develop invasive breast cancer throughout their lifetime. (American Cancer Society, 2023) * For 2023, an estimated 297,790 new cases of invasive breast cancer and 55,720 new cases of noninvasive breast cancer will be diagnosed.

- More cases are being found in women in their 20s and 30s.

- Men can get breast cancer, too. While it is rare, about 1 in 833 men will develop the disease.

- Hormone-driven cancers are common. Many breast cancers feed on estrogen and progesterone, which have implications for birth control, hormone replacement therapy (HRT), and even certain supplements.

Breast Cancer in Men: The Often-Overlooked Reality

For cis men, trans men, and anyone who needs to know: you belong in this conversation.

Breast cancer doesn't only happen to women. While it's less common, men are diagnosed too. If you're reading this because you've heard the words "you have breast cancer," I'm sorry you're here. Many men describe the diagnosis as shocking, even surreal—especially when they're told how rare it is. One man on a patient forum described his experience: *I was 39, and the odds were 1 in 500,000. I couldn't believe it was me.*

That rarity can feel isolating. Even the clinical environment can make it worse—forms that only list "female," pink waiting rooms, and pamphlets that don't mention men at all. As one patient put it, "Even the paperwork makes you feel like you don't exist." You do exist. Your story matters.

You may be carrying fears that aren't always voiced: Will treatment affect how I see myself as a man? What about intimacy, dating, or the scars I'll carry? One man asked, "Do the scars and fake boobs make me undatable?" These questions are real, and you're not alone in asking them.

Men account for 1% of all breast cancer cases.

- The lifetime risk for men is about 1 in 833. (American Cancer Society, 2023). In 2023, about 2,800 new cases are expected.

- Higher mortality rates—this is not because it's deadlier, but because it's diagnosed later.

- Most cases are hormone receptor-positive. This means treatments like Tamoxifen can be effective.

Advocacy Tip #1: Men should check for unusual lumps, swelling, or discharge from the nipple—and should push for screening if they have a family history of breast cancer.

If you're reading this as a partner, son, brother, or friend: your life has been altered, too. Supporting someone through cancer can feel like walking on shifting ground. You may not always know what to say or do, and that's okay. What matters most is that you keep showing up.

This book was written with women in mind, but the guidance, tools, and resilience reminders apply to you, too. Whether you are a man with breast cancer, a trans man navigating new complexities, or a male caregiver standing beside someone you love, you belong in this conversation. Trans women and nonbinary people may also face unique screening and diagnostic challenges. Talk with your healthcare provider about personalized risk and screening guidelines.

Younger Women and Breast Cancer: What You Need to Know

While breast cancer is more common in women over 40, it is not just a disease of postmenopausal women. While breast cancer risk increases with age, it's increasingly being diagnosed in younger women, often with more aggressive types.

About 4% of invasive breast cancers are diagnosed in women under 40.* About 9% of all new breast cancer cases in the U.S. are found in women younger than 45 (American Cancer Society, 2023).

- Younger women are less likely to be screened early. Mammograms are usually recommended starting at age 40, but younger women may not get checked until symptoms appear.

- Denser breast tissue makes detection harder. Tumors can be more difficult to detect in mammograms for younger women.

- More aggressive subtypes. Younger patients are more likely to be diagnosed with triple-negative breast cancer, which doesn't respond to hormone therapy and often requires chemotherapy.

- Higher recurrence risk. Breast cancer in younger women is more likely to come back after treatment.

Advocacy Tip #2: If something feels wrong, push for testing. Do not let a doctor dismiss your concerns just because you are "too young" for breast cancer. If you have a lump, a change in breast shape, persistent pain, or any other abnormal symptoms, insist on imaging (ultrasound, mammogram, or MRI).

Racial and Ethnic Disparities

- Breast cancer incidence rates vary among racial and ethnic groups. * Black women have a higher incidence rate before age 40.

- Black women are more likely to die from breast cancer at any age. This is due to a combination of factors, including later-stage diagnosis and more aggressive tumor types. (American Cancer Society, 2023)

- Black women under 35 have breast cancer incidence rates twice as high and mortality rates three times as high as white women in the same age group.

Chapter 20: The Myth of One Disease

"One in eight women will face breast cancer." It's a number we hear so often that it almost becomes background noise. Here's what that statistic doesn't tell you: breast cancer isn't one disease. It isn't a single diagnosis with a single treatment. It's a complicated family of conditions, each with its own language, risks, and options.

People often compare stories: *"My mom didn't have chemo." "My friend was on a different drug." "Are you sure your doctor gave you the right treatment?"* These comments usually come from a good place. Still, they miss the reality: two people can share the same diagnosis label—*Stage II breast cancer*, for example—and still need completely different treatments.

The Biology Beneath the Diagnosis

The first layer of complexity lives in your tumor's biology. Doctors test for three key receptors: estrogen (ER), progesterone (PR), and HER2. Each can be positive or negative, so there are 8 possible combinations—ranging from triple positive to triple negative.

(See Figure on the next page: Hormone Receptor Decision Tree with Approximate U.S. Distribution.) This visual illustrates how receptor status is categorized and why specific categories, such as triple-negative or triple-positive, are frequently discussed.

Hormone Receptor (HR) Tree with Approximate US Distribution

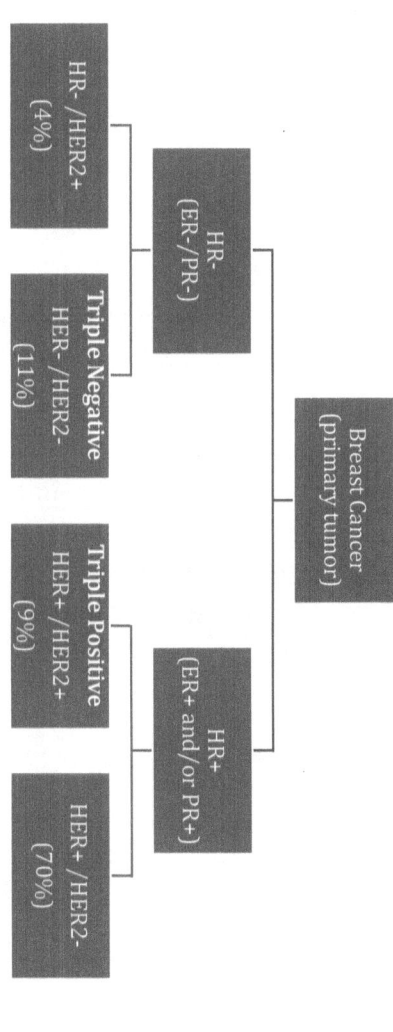

After testing for **hormone receptors (ER/PR)** and **HER2** (aka HER2neu), most U.S. cases fall into HR+/HER2– (~70%), with smaller groups HR+/HER2+ (~9%), HR–/HER2+ (~4%), and HR–/HER2–/triple-negative (~11%). Proportions vary by population and do not include ~6% 'unknown' subtypes (SEER 2018–2022).

Note: "Hormone receptor positive" (HR+) means the tumor has estrogen (ER) and/or progesterone (PR) receptors. Most HR+ cancers are ER+ and PR+, but some are ER+ only or PR+ only. All are generally treated as HR+ because they may respond to hormone-blocking therapies.

Source: SEER incidence distributions, 2018–2022 (National Cancer Institute, 2023).

157

And that's just the starting point. Beyond receptors, tumors can be grouped into molecular subtypes like Luminal A, Luminal B, HER2-enriched, or basal-like. Add in tumor grade, Ki-67 (a measure of how quickly the cells are dividing), and genetic mutations like BRCA1, BRCA2, or PIK3CA, and no two cancers look the same under a microscope.

Stage Is Only the Beginning

When people hear "Stage II," they often assume that means the same thing for everyone. But stage only measures how far the cancer has spread, not how aggressive it is or how it might respond to drugs.

One woman's Stage II might be a slow-growing, estrogen-driven cancer that responds beautifully to hormone therapy. Another woman's Stage II could be a fast-moving, triple-negative tumor that requires aggressive chemotherapy right away. Same stage, radically different stories.

The Treatment Tree

Once your biology and stage are clear, the treatment decision tree begins. There isn't one fixed menu—there are dozens of paths.

Surgery might mean a lumpectomy, mastectomy, or even a double mastectomy.

Chemotherapy could be given before surgery (to shrink the tumor) or after, and the drug combinations vary: AC-T, TC, CMF, and others.

Targeted therapies are tailored to receptor status. HER2-positive cancers may be treated with trastuzumab, pertuzumab, or Kadcyla.

Hormone therapy for ER+ cancers could mean Tamoxifen, aromatase inhibitors, or ovarian suppression—sometimes for five to ten years.

Radiation is necessary for some women, optional for others, and not recommended at all for a different group.

Immunotherapy is now available for some triple-negative cancers.

Additional drugs, such as bone-strengtheners or PARP inhibitors, may enter the mix.

Even the same drug isn't "the same" across patients: doses change, schedules differ, and side effects may force switches or pauses.

Survivorship and the Long Tail of Treatment

Treatment doesn't always end when the last infusion is over, or the last radiation beam is delivered. For many women, the journey stretches years into survivorship. Hormone therapy can last five to ten years. Scans and bloodwork become part of routine life. Side effects such as joint pain, bone loss, lymphedema, or fatigue require ongoing management. Survivorship is its own chapter of breast cancer—different from active treatment, but still shaped by the diagnosis.

The First Month: Drinking From a Fire Hose

If all of this sounds overwhelming, it's because it *is*. The first month after diagnosis feels like drinking from a fire hose.

You start with biopsy results, then proceed to receptor testing, and finally to genetic testing. Scans may follow—MRI, CT, and bone scans. One day, you're meeting a surgeon, the next an oncologist, and then a radiation specialist. Each appointment brings new words, new options, and sometimes new changes to the plan you thought was already set.

No wonder so many women describe those early weeks as a blur.

The next page shows a snapshot of what those first 30 days often include. Your exact order and pace may differ, but seeing the bigger picture can help you prepare for what's ahead.

What A Typical First Month Might Look Like

Day 1-5 Diagnosis

Biopsy results (core needle or surgical biopsy) → confirms cancer type.

Pathology report: ER/PR/HER2 testing begins.

Emotional crash + first round of phone calls to family/friends.

Day 5-10 Imaging & Staging

Breast MRI and/or diagnostic mammogram (to check extent in breast).

Ultrasound of axilla (underarm) to check lymph nodes.

Possible CT, PET, or bone scan if concern about spread.

Referral to breast surgeon and medical oncologist.

Day 10-15 Genetic Testing

Genetic counseling session.

Genetic testing panel (BRCA1, BRCA2, PIK3CA, PALB2, etc.).

Baseline blood tests (CBC, liver/kidney function).

Fertility counseling/referral (if premenopausal and desired).

Day 15-20 Specialist Consults

Consult with breast surgeon: discussion of lumpectomy vs. mastectomy.

Consult with medical oncologist: chemotherapy vs. targeted therapy.

Consult with radiation oncologist (if lumpectomy or nodes involved).

Echocardiogram (baseline heart function if HER2+ or chemo likely; (National Comprehensive Cancer Network [NCCN], 2025; U.S. Food and Drug Administration, 2025).

Day 20-30 Treatment Planning

Second opinions (if sought).

Multidisciplinary tumor board (in some centers).

Pre-surgical clearance / pre-chemo clearance.

Central port placement scheduled (if chemo anticipated).

Day 25-30 Treatment Plan Finalized

Surgery date set (if surgery first).

OR chemotherapy start date (if neoadjuvant chemo first).

Radiation usually sequenced later, but plan outlined.

Introduction to nurse navigator, social worker, or patient support services.

Note for patients: Not all of this happens in the same order, and sometimes the "first 30 days" stretches longer depending on scheduling, insurance approvals, and second opinions. But most people will go through **biopsy confirmation → receptor testing → staging imaging → genetic testing → consults → treatment plan decision** in that first month.

The Science Doesn't Stand Still

Adding another layer of complexity: the science is constantly evolving. Thousands of breast cancer studies are published every year. Some are small, but others directly change what doctors recommend in the clinic.

In just the past five years alone, dozens of new drugs have changed how breast cancer is treated. That means the treatment your mother received ten years ago—or even the treatment a friend received three years ago—may already be outdated. Doctors must continually read, learn, and adjust.

Clinical Trials and Research Access

For some women, clinical trials become part of their treatment. Trials are where the newest therapies are tested, and they give patients access to drugs years before they may become widely available. Clinical trials also remind us that breast cancer treatment isn't static—it's moving forward every day. Participation depends on where you live, what's available, and whether your oncologist connects you to those opportunities.

Equity and Access

Access matters too. A woman treated at a major urban cancer center may be offered options—advanced imaging, targeted drugs, or clinical trials—that aren't available in a rural hospital. Insurance, geography, and even cultural barriers can shape the plan. Two women with the same diagnosis may receive very different treatments simply because of where they live or the system they're navigating.

Why No Two Journeys Are Alike

When you stack all of this together—the biology, the stage, the treatment options, the evolving science—you can see why no two journeys are alike. But it's not just the science. Personal choices matter too: fertility goals, quality-of-life considerations, risk tolerance, and other health conditions. Geography and access to care matter. Support systems matter.

And layered over all of this is emotion. Some women choose a double mastectomy even when a lumpectomy would be equally safe, because the peace of mind matters more than the statistics. Others may decline aggressive treatment because quality of life feels like the higher priority. These choices are deeply personal, and they remind us that cancer isn't only about biology—it's also about the human being making decisions in the middle of fear, hope, and uncertainty.

So when someone says, *"That's not what my mom had,"* or *"Are you sure your doctor put you on the right meds?"*— remember: they're comparing apples to oranges. Breast cancer isn't one thing, and your treatment plan was built for you.

Validation and Perspective

If you felt overwhelmed at the start, you weren't failing— you were responding normally to an abnormal amount of information. Breast cancer is complex. That complexity can feel frightening, but it also means more options, more personalized care, and more hope than ever before.

No two women have the same journey. I have yet to meet anyone with my exact treatment plan. Each of us learns that we don't have to walk it alone. Or ride in the lifeboat unattended. I imagine my cancer journey as a river. When we first get in the lifeboat at the time of diagnosis, we're on our backs, staring at the sky, trusting that the practitioners have put us in the right boat with the appropriate provisions. As we move forward, we slowly start to sit up and see where we're going. We stop at more ports of call, start asking more detailed questions, and, in some cases, begin steering our boat. By the time we get to the bottom of the river, some of us can step out of the boat and return to living with cancer behind us. For others, the river winds on. Their journey is longer, often without a final landing point. However, it is still full of moments of steering, living, resting, and finding support along the way.

Chapter 21: Advocating for Yourself in the Healthcare System

As a patient, it can be easy to feel like you are just a breast, a blood test, or a cluster of tissues—a set of numbers on a chart rather than a whole person. But you are a whole person. Your body is an interconnected system, and you deserve care that treats you as such. The best practitioners understand this. My acupuncturist, for example, always treated all of me, not just the side effects of my cancer. However, not every provider sees the bigger picture, which means you have to advocate for yourself.

Speaking Up When Something Feels Off

After my knee injury, I had to fight for the proper care—navigating insurance, pushing for sports medicine physical therapy (PT) versus standard PT, and making sure I got what I needed. It was a crash course in advocacy.

Cancer? That was advocacy on overdrive. Every step required vigilance: understanding my treatment options; pushing back when something didn't feel right; and demanding answers. There's this unspoken expectation that cancer patients should be docile and that we should trust the process. But I learned quickly that survival required something else entirely. It meant speaking up, questioning, and insisting.

Your Lungs: Don't Ignore Breathing Changes

Radiation treatment is precise but demanding. During each session, I had to hold my breath perfectly still while the laser lights aligned with the tiny dot tattoos on my torso. Luckily, the process was quick, often taking less time than it took to undress, wait, and get dressed again.

Despite these precautions, there's always a risk of collateral damage. After treatment, a scan revealed damage to the top of my left lung. This was especially alarming given that I had already suffered a **blood** clot in my lung during chemo. I started walking again to rebuild strength, but my heart rate soared to 175 after just a few uphill steps in my hilly neighborhood. I was clinging to trees, gasping for air, unable to expand my lungs.

I repeatedly voiced my concerns, but my providers brushed them aside. They were not worried, but I was. So, I kept pushing. Finally, I asked my oncology PA:

"What do you see when you look at me? Am I just a boob or a blood test, or do you see all of me?"

That question changed everything. The physician's assistant immediately referred me to a pulmonologist. That same day, I had an appointment. The pulmonologist confirmed that the lung damage was not life-threatening, and I just needed to keep moving, rebuild stamina, and trust that I wasn't about to have a heart attack walking up stairs. Had I accepted dismissal the first time I brought it up, I would have spent months worrying rather than working toward recovery.

***Advocacy Tip #3:** If something feels off, say so. Keep pushing until you get an answer that makes sense. Your voice matters. Your concerns matter.*

Your Balance: Pay Attention and Speak Up

My balance had already been compromised years before my cancer diagnosis. My 2009 injury had partially destroyed my peroneal nerve, leaving me with permanent foot drop on my left side. I wear an ankle-foot orthosis (AFO) daily and must be cautious about activities that require fast movements or twisting.

Then, during my second round of Kadcyla chemo, no one recommended that I freeze my fingers and toes to prevent neuropathy. As a result, I developed it. Several toes and fingertips on my right side became completely numb. It wasn't painful, but it was dangerous.

One day, during a Pilates plank on the reformer, I unknowingly bent a toe under my foot and broke it, because I couldn't feel it.

I knew I needed help, so I pushed for a referral to neuro-physical therapy. That decision changed everything. My therapist tailored my exercises to my unique challenges, helping me rebuild strength and confidence. Because of her, I can still walk in the woods, practice Pilates, and live the active life I want, instead of letting cancer and treatment take that away from me.

Advocacy Tip #4: If you're struggling with balance, neuropathy, or weakness, ask for a neuro-physical therapy referral. Don't wait for someone to suggest it. You know your body best.

How to Advocate for the Best Care

1. **See Yourself as a Whole Person—And Expect Your Doctors to Do the Same.**

   Cancer affects every part of your body and life. Don't be afraid to bring up concerns unrelated to your primary treatment. You are more than a tumor.

2. **Don't Let Dismissal Stop You**

   If a doctor shrugs off your symptoms, but you still feel something is wrong, ask again. Get a second opinion. Demand an explanation. Persistence is key.

3. **Ask for the Right Specialist.**

   Your oncologist is not your only doctor. If you're experiencing symptoms outside their expertise—like breathing issues, balance struggles, or nerve pain—ask for a pulmonologist, physical therapist, neurologist, or other specialist who can address the issue directly.

4. **Trust Yourself.**

   You know when something isn't right. Keep pushing for answers until you get the care you deserve.

Cancer treatment is hard enough without having to fight to be heard. But you must. Keep speaking up. Keep asking questions. Keep advocating. Because at the end of the day, no one will fight for your body the way you will.

I've included a detailed list of questions you may want to ask your doctors in the resources section (Chapter 35). Don't worry about memorizing them all now—you can return to that list when you're ready.

Chapter 22: Resilience and Emotional Health

In Section Two, you read resilience stories from women who found ways to keep going when life pulled the rug out from under them. This chapter builds on those stories by looking inward—at the emotional health side of resilience. Cancer doesn't just test the body; it tests our expectations, our relationships, and the way we talk to ourselves. Here, I share moments that taught me to let go of guilt, to communicate more clearly with caregivers, and to quiet the "mean girl" voice in my head. My hope is that these examples and tools give you practical ways to reframe guilt, reduce stress, and protect your emotional energy when it feels like you have none to spare.

Framing Expectations and Reducing Stress with Family and Caregivers

I laugh now when I think about my "clean underwear" moment during chemo, but at the time, it was a turning point for me. I struggled with guilt throughout my cancer journey — guilt about what I couldn't do, guilt about leaning so heavily on my husband, Gus, guilt about everything I wasn't managing.

By my twelfth weekly treatment, I was wrecked. I had spent more hours than I care to count in the bathroom, my energy was gone, and I was still recovering from a pulmonary embolism that had delayed one of my infusions. I couldn't keep up with everyday life anymore. Laundry piled up. The house didn't look like it used to. All the little projects I used to manage on autopilot sat untouched.

One day, I sat on the couch and confessed to Gus how guilty I felt. He was working so hard to keep everything running — for us and for his mom, who was battling illness in another state — while I was slogging through chemo and barely functioning. I told him I felt bad about the laundry piling up, worried he'd see me as slacking or not trying hard enough.

He looked me dead in the eye and asked one simple question:

"Do you have clean underwear?"

I said, "Yes."

"Good," he said. "So, do I. Then who cares? The laundry isn't hurting anybody. It'll get done when you're ready to do it — or when I'm ready to do it. Until then, it can wait."

I burst out laughing. It was so simple, but it cut straight through the guilt I'd been carrying.

Later, I teased him and asked, "What if I *didn't* have clean underwear?" Without missing a beat, Gus grinned and said, "Then I'd tell you to buy yourself some new ones. Something nice."

That was it. No drama. No guilt. No subtle scorekeeping. Just love, humor, and permission to let go of what didn't matter in that moment.

When Expectations Collide

Not every conversation goes like this. In fact, I've seen and experienced plenty where it doesn't.

Cancer treatment forces everyone into new roles without a roadmap. Patients are suddenly balancing survival, exhaustion, fear, and shifts in their identity. Partners and caregivers are juggling logistics, financial stress, and their own grief. Family and friends want to help, but they don't always know how.

When nobody talks openly about expectations, misalignment creeps in fast.

I've read dozens of stories from other women going through treatment, and one thread struck me deeply. A woman had just finished four brutal rounds of AC and was gearing up for twelve weeks of Taxol. She'd kept up as much as she could — driving her son, making appointments, cleaning when she had energy. She was finally starting to feel hopeful that the next phase might be lighter.

Then her significant other dropped a bomb: *"You need to start doing more."*

She spiraled. She'd been surviving on fumes, giving everything she had, and in the moment she felt most proud for making it through AC, someone she loved told her it wasn't enough. That comment hit hard, leaving her questioning herself, her relationship, and her worth.

I see this over and over again:

- Patients internalize guilt and shame, thinking they're failing their loved ones.

- Caregivers feel overwhelmed and resentful, sometimes without realizing it.

- Both sides assume the other "should just know" what's needed.

That's a recipe for arguments on top of exhaustion. This is where communication starts to break down—when we assume the other person understands what's possible without explaining it. One of the best tools I've found to make this visible is the *Spoon Theory* (Miserandino, 2003).

The Spoon Theory: Making Energy Visible

I didn't invent this idea, but I wish I had because it's brilliant. Christine Miserandino, who lives with lupus, came up with the Spoon Theory to explain her limited energy to her friend. She grabbed a handful of spoons from the table and said, "Okay, imagine you start the day with these twelve spoons. Each thing you do costs one or more spoons — showering, getting dressed, making breakfast, driving to an appointment."

By mid-morning, you might already be down to four spoons. By the afternoon, maybe two. And you don't get any extras.

Cancer treatment works the same way. You only have so many spoons to spend each day. Some days you wake up with five. Some days you wake up with one. The trick is to budget your spoons intentionally, so you don't run out by noon.

This framework also helps caregivers understand why you can't "just do more." If you only have three spoons today and chemo takes two of them, skipping laundry isn't laziness— it's energy math.

You can literally make this visual. Write "spoons" on sticky notes and move them from "available" to "spent" throughout the day. Or text your caregiver: "I've got one spoon left today — want me to spend it on laundry or talking to you?" It makes invisible fatigue visible, and it can completely change conversations about expectations.

Why Misalignment Happens

This isn't about bad intentions — it's about different realities colliding.

For patients:

- Your job is survival. Energy is rationed. Every spoon counts.

- You might "look fine" on the outside, but inside, your body is working overtime just to process the drugs they're putting through your veins.

- You want to protect your loved ones from carrying the burden, so you minimize your needs until resentment creeps in silently.

For caregivers and family:

- You're adjusting to a new normal, too. Sometimes you don't know what's helpful versus intrusive.

- You're balancing fear, frustration, and your own stress while trying to hold everything together.

- If your loved one "looks okay, it's easy to assume they *are* okay.

Nobody is the villain here. But when we don't communicate what's realistic, it's too easy for hurt feelings, guilt, and resentment to build up on both sides.

What Gus Got Right

Back to the clean underwear moment. Gus did three things beautifully — and they're lessons anyone can borrow:

1. **He prioritized what counted.**
   Clean underwear mattered to me. Perfectly folded laundry didn't matter to him.

2. **He removed guilt from the equation.**
   There was no "you should" or "why haven't you."
   Just acceptance of where we were.

3. **He used humor to release pressure.**
   His "buy new underwear" line gave me permission
   to laugh at something that had been weighing me
   down. And see an alternative I hadn't seen before.

That combination — clarity, compassion, and humor — kept
us aligned.

From Guilt to Grace: A Framework for Resetting Expectations

Suppose I had to distill what works best for patients and
caregivers. In that case, it comes down to one shift: **replace
silent assumptions with small, honest conversations.**

Here's a tool I've started sharing with others going through
treatment:

Step 1. Name Your Capacity

"Here's what I *can* manage this week. Here's what I
can't."

Step 2. Ask Without Apology

"I need help with driving to appointments and
keeping up with groceries this week. Would you be
able to cover those?"

Step 3. Check in on Caregiver Capacity Too

"What's feeling heavy for you right now? Where do
you need support?"

Step 4. Focus on What Actually Matters

Decide what's essential and let the rest go. Clean
underwear, feeding the dog, ensuring the kids are

dropped off at school, and making it to appointments —those count. Messy floors and unfinished projects don't. Protect your spoons for what matters most.

Key Takeaway

When patients and caregivers are out of sync, minor frustrations turn into big wounds. But with a bit of intentionality, grace, and humor, you can reduce the stress of cancer's "second job": managing expectations.

Sometimes, it really is as simple as asking, "Do we both have clean underwear?" If the answer is yes, everything else can wait.

Chapter 23: Practical Tools for Aligning Expectations

Cancer treatment turns your entire life upside down — and yet somehow, laundry, bills, carpool schedules, and grocery lists don't get the memo. Without clear communication, you can end up frustrated, misunderstood, and carrying guilt that doesn't belong to you.

This section provides simple frameworks to help you reset expectations with family and caregivers, allowing everyone to breathe a little easier.

1. Scripts for Hard Conversations

Sometimes you're too tired to craft the perfect words. Here are a few to lean on when you need them:

For Patients: When You Feel Pressured to "Do More"

- "I know it might look like I'm okay, but my body's still recovering, and I'm pacing myself. I promise I'll take on more when I have energy. For now, I need your help focusing on what matters most."

- "I want to do more when I can, but my energy isn't consistent right now. Could we sit down and make a list together of what's essential versus what can wait?"

- "I'm not ignoring what needs to be done — I'm prioritizing healing. If specific things are stressing you out, let's talk about those and figure out a plan."

For Caregivers: When You're Feeling Overwhelmed

- "I want to support you, and I also need us to share the load in a way that works for both of us. Can we talk about which things I can take on and which we can let go of for now?"

- "I'm noticing I'm getting stressed trying to manage everything. Would you be okay if we asked a friend, family member, or neighbor to step in with meals or errands?"

- "I want to help you without guessing what you need. Can you tell me the two or three things that would be most helpful this week?"

These scripts foster collaboration rather than conflict. They shift the conversation away from accusations ("you're not doing enough") and toward problem-solving ("how can we do this together?").

2. The Weekly Check-In: A 10-Minute Reset

This is one of the most effective tools I've seen for keeping patients and caregivers aligned without endless, exhausting conversations. It's a quick, structured touchpoint to reduce stress and prevent resentment from building.

How it works: Pick one day a week. Sit down together for ten minutes.

Answer these four questions.

1. **Energy Check:** What went well this week? What felt hard?

2. **Top Priority:** What's most important for us to handle this week?

3. **Ask & Offer:**

    a. Patient: Here's what I need.

    b. Caretaker: Here's what I can take on.

4. **Adjustments:**

    a. What's one thing we can let go of, ask our friends to do, or simplify to make this week easier?

That's it. No overexplaining. No defending yourself. Just a short, simple reset.

3. The "Help Menu."

One of the most significant stress points in caregiving is the dreaded guessing game. Friends and family want to help, but patients often hesitate to ask, and caregivers don't always know what's most useful.

Create a Help Menu — a short list of tasks where others can pitch in without endless coordination. Keep it somewhere visible, like a whiteboard, fridge, or a shared note on your phone.

Sample Help Menu:

- Driving to appointments
- Picking up prescriptions
- Dropping off groceries
- Walking the dog
- Doing a load of laundry
- Sending a funny text or meme when you're too tired to talk

This shifts the dynamic from "nagging" to "choosing." Instead of pushing each other, you're inviting help where it matters.

4. Green, Yellow, Red: The Energy Language

One of the simplest ways to manage expectations is to communicate energy levels without overexplaining. It removes the guilt spiral and replaces it with a shared shorthand:

- **Green Day:** Feeling steady, might handle a couple of small tasks, maybe even a walk.

- **Yellow Day:** Energy is unpredictable; choose one priority, skip the rest.

- **Red Day:** Full rest mode. Survival and healing only.

Caregivers can check in with: "Green, yellow, or red today?"

Patients can respond with one word. No defending. No guilt. It opens space for empathy instead of misunderstanding.

5. When Expectations Still Clash

Even with scripts, weekly check-ins, and color-coded energy updates, conflict will still happen sometimes. It's normal. Here's how to navigate those more challenging moments:

1. **Pause, don't react.** Take a breath before responding in the heat of the moment.

2. **Name what's really going on.** Often, the fight isn't about dishes or laundry — it's about fear, exhaustion, or feeling unseen.

3. **Use the "Calling In" Approach** *(explained below).*

4. **Get outside support if needed.** Oncologists, nurse navigators, therapists, social workers, and support groups can help mediate tricky dynamics.

The Calling In Approach

When someone says something hurtful — even unintentionally — you have two options: you can **call them out** or **call them in**.

- **Calling out** = reacting sharply, often escalating tension.

- **Calling in** = inviting the person into the conversation with compassion and curiosity.

Why this matters: Cancer pushes everyone to their limits. Sometimes caregivers snap out of frustration, and sometimes patients lash out from pain. "Calling in" creates space to **repair, not rupture.**

Example:

- **Calling Out:** "You have no idea what I'm going through. Stop telling me to do more!"

- **Calling In:** "I know you want to help, but when I hear 'do more,' it feels like I'm failing. Can we talk about what's realistic for both of us right now?"

This approach reduces defensiveness and maintains a focus on working together instead of against each other. It doesn't mean ignoring hurt feelings — it means choosing language that protects the relationship **and** solves the problem.

Expectation Setting Is Crucial

Cancer already asks so much of you. You don't need to carry the extra weight of guilt, resentment, or mismatched expectations. When you focus on what actually matters, communicate openly, and give each other grace, you create space for healing — together.

And if you both have clean underwear? You're already doing enough.

Chapter 24: For Those Living with Metastatic Breast Cancer

Resilience When the Goal Isn't Cure

Not everyone who reads this book will be in remission. Some of you are reading this while living with metastatic breast cancer—also called MBC or Stage IV. That means the cancer has spread beyond your breast and lymph nodes to other parts of your body. It also means your treatment may never fully stop.

Maybe your diagnosis came out of nowhere. Perhaps it was a recurrence. Maybe you're living scan to scan, or you're years into treatment and baffling every prediction. This section is for you.

Let's be clear: This isn't about false hope.

This isn't about pretending you're fine, nor is it about pushing positivity. It's about acknowledging your reality *without* collapsing under it.

You already know the stats. You already know what Google says. What you *may not* hear enough is this:

You are still here.
You are still in charge of your story.
You still get to *live.*

What Resilience Might Look Like for You

Resilience in your case may not mean "bouncing back" or trying to feel "normal" again.

It might mean:

- Living fully while also grieving honestly
- Making meaning without toxic cheerleading
- Claiming agency where you can, and softness where you need it

Here are tools that may help—not to erase pain, but to anchor you in your humanity:

Name What You Can Control

You can't control your scans.

You can control how you spend your good days.

You can choose how to explain your reality to others.

You can decide who gets access to your time, energy, and truth.

Even small choices, such as the music you play during infusions, the socks you wear, or when you say "no," can become acts of power.

Create Legacy on Your Terms

If this idea feels empowering, not grim, consider:

- Writing letters or recording videos for loved ones
- Making a playlist of songs that remind you of each child or friend
- Assembling a memory box or passing down a recipe with a story
- Planning your own celebration, your own damn way

Legacy work isn't about giving up. It's about making space for *you* to be remembered the way you want to be.

Plan for Later, Even While Living Now

Having an advance directive or end-of-life preferences written down doesn't mean you're surrendering. It means you're choosing clarity over chaos. It's a gift to yourself and your people. When my father unexpectedly died in a plane crash, his estate was a mess. His will wasn't up-to-date, and he hadn't given much thought to how he'd like his estate handled. It became a 12-year slog for those of us left behind. Receiving the dreaded white with green triangle full-page envelopes from the lawyers in the mailbox and paying the attorneys' fees out of what he had left behind.

You can plan quietly, gradually, or in a single afternoon. Making sure your loved ones have the time and space to grieve and aren't focused on filing your estate's tax return is a gift you have control over after you've passed.

Find People Who Get It

There are whole communities of women living with MBC who *don't* want empty slogans. They want real talk. They like dark humor. They want to be seen.

If you're feeling alone, want to talk to other women who get it, or want to pass along what you've learned and be a mentor to others, you might look into:

- **METAvivor** – Research, support, and advocacy for people with MBC

- **Living Beyond Breast Cancer** (LBBC) – Offers MBC-specific programs and communities

- **Instagram creators and bloggers** who share their daily lives with MBC honestly and openly.

Give Yourself Permission to Feel It All

You don't have to be brave every day. You don't have to be "grateful it's not worse." You don't have to radiate strength for the comfort of others. You're allowed to have messy days. Enraged days. Peaceful days. Quiet, boring, unremarkable days where nothing hurts and no one asks how you are. That counts, too.

One Last Thing

If no one's said this to you lately:

- I'm glad you're still here. Your voice matters. Your presence matters. Your life, *as it is*, is worth honoring.

- You may live five more months. You may live five more years. You may keep baffling your doctors and breaking actuarial charts.

- No matter how much time you have left, what you do with it is yours to decide.

Chapter 25: When You're Not Feeling Nice: What to Say When People Won't Listen

There will be days when you have no energy left for grace. When you're not feeling patient or diplomatic. When one more "at least" or "you're so strong" will make you snap. You'll encounter that person in the waiting room or in line at the pharmacy or the DMV. You'll be shocked by the brazen statements. My favorite was from the DMV line.

Unfortunately, I had to get my RealID before my hair had fully grown back in. It was just long enough that I was comfortable going out in public without a wig or a hat. It was still warm here in Oregon in early October of 2023. So I was not-so-patiently waiting to get my picture taken when a woman said to me, "I wish I had the nerve to wear my hair that short."

I was flabbergasted at first. Was it a compliment? Was it a comment on her own vanity? Was it an insult? I couldn't quite parse her meaning. And I didn't really want to know more about her or her hairstyle wishes.

Welcome to that part of cancer no one warns you about: the mental load of managing *other people's reactions to your diagnosis and appearance.*

This section isn't about being mean. It's about boundaries, tone, and calling out unhelpful behavior—because sometimes that's the only way to protect your peace.

You get to have days when you're not "grateful."

You get to shut people down.

You get to use your sharp tongue if you need to.

There's a version of you that's calm, generous, and patient.

This section isn't for her.

This is for the version of you who is nauseous, sleep-deprived, emotionally threadbare, bald, queasy, sick, and *done* with managing other people's feelings while you're just trying to survive. Because here's the thing: sometimes it's not *your* attitude that needs adjusting. Sometimes it's the people around you who are showing up all wrong.

And sometimes, the only way they'll get it is if you say something sharp.

You're allowed to protect your energy.

You're allowed to use your words as a boundary.

You're allowed to not be nice.

Why This Happens (And Why It's Exhausting)

We covered what toxic positivity is. Here's what it *feels* like in the wild: being bombarded with unasked-for advice, sugarcoated clichés, or someone else's attempt to tie a bow around your pain. People often mean well—yet intentions don't always equal impact. If you haven't already, you're about to get unsolicited advice and endless questions on top of everything else.

Everything said to you may sound harmless at first. You don't owe anyone a TED Talk on your diagnosis. You don't have to soften your voice to make someone else comfortable. These one-liners are here for when you need a fast way to protect your peace—without a PowerPoint.

Ask yourself:

- Are they trying to fix my feelings instead of hearing them?

- Are they more focused on *their* discomfort than my reality?

- Do I feel dismissed or silenced after the conversation?

If the answer is yes, toxic positivity is in the room.

What You Can Say Instead of Smiling and Nodding

You don't owe anyone an explanation. If you feel the need to speak up—either to protect your energy or call someone in—here are some ideas. Some are snarky, some are kind. Some help you set a clear boundary. Pick the ones you need and keep them close. You never know when you'll need them in line at the grocery store or when trying to get your photo ID updated.

One-Liners to Shut It Down

When they question your treatment choices:
- "I'm not taking questions on my treatment today."
- "That's a private decision between me and my medical team."
- "My doctor and I are aligned. That's all anyone needs to know."
- "My oncologist trusts the tumor board. I trust them. That's the whole story."
- "Thanks, but I'm not looking for feedback."
- "Chemo sucks. So does cancer coming back. I picked the suck I can survive."

When they compare you to someone else:
- "Glad it worked out for your cousin. I'm doing what's right for me."

- "Every cancer story is different. Mine's not up for debate."

When they say "at least" or something dismissive:

- "I know you're trying to help, but that comment feels minimizing."

- "It's not helpful to be told to be positive when I'm in pain."

- "I know you mean well, but your comment makes it harder for me to cope."

- "I'm already doing something hard. Please don't make it harder."

- "Telling me to 'stay positive' doesn't make this go away. It just makes me feel more alone."

When you want to walk away gracefully:

- "I don't want to talk about cancer right now."

- "Let's change the subject—I'm trying to hold onto what little energy I've got."

For the truly fed up:

- "My PET is clean. My doctors still want chemo. Your opinion isn't in the treatment plan."

- "Did you mean to be helpful? Because that wasn't."

- "Please don't confuse my silence with agreement. I'm out of energy."

- "This isn't up for discussion."

- "That comment wasn't helpful. Please don't say that again."

- "I know you mean well. I need you to stop."

Gentle but firm:

- "I'm following medical advice. That's the full story."

- "Thanks for your concern—let's talk about something else."
- "I'm not up for explaining today."

Snarky:

- "Did you go to medical school since I last saw you?"
- "I'm already tired from cancer. Explaining my choices would finish me off."
- "Chemo's bad, but unsolicited opinions? Brutal."
- "If I had a dollar for every unsolicited opinion, I could pay off my medical bills."
- "Thanks for the pep talk. I'll go ahead and feel my actual feelings anyway."
- "I know you mean well. I need presence, not positivity."

If You Snapped and Feel Guilty

Welcome to being human. If someone caught you on a chemo-cranky day and you bit their head off? You're not a villain. If they deserved it, oh well. If they didn't—apologize if it feels right, then let it go. You're doing your best with very little fuel.

Boundaries aren't rude. They're how you stay upright. You don't owe gentle when you're exhausted. You don't owe pretty when you're in pain. You owe yourself peace.

You're Not Rude—You're Real

Not everyone deserves access to your story. Not everyone can handle your truth. And some people will never understand how much harm they're doing with their good intentions.

Let them be uncomfortable. You've got bigger things to handle. Like living. Like healing. Like protecting your peace.

Chapter 26: Asking for Help: Confronting Guilt, Anger, and the "Mean Girl" in My Head

As someone who prides herself on being strong and capable, admitting I needed help during treatment was not easy. But I quickly realized I could not face the overwhelming emotions and uncertainties alone. I contacted the cancer center's therapist, who specialized in working with patients like me.

Support groups were an option, but I knew they were not the right fit. Not because I couldn't relate to the other members, but because I would relate *too much*. My years as a career advisor and counselor meant I was trained to focus on others. I knew I would worry about everyone else in the group instead of myself. What I needed wasn't a group dynamic. I needed a guide to help me navigate my own emotional minefield, which lay ahead.

My therapist was fantastic. She was young, energetic, and passionate, with a long black ponytail that swayed as she spoke. She gave me tactical and practical advice in just three sessions, which I needed. She was the one who recommended books such as *"When Life Hits Hard"* by Russ Harris. She helped me focus on caring for myself during the most challenging part of the journey: the beginning.

At that stage, everything felt uncertain. I did not yet know the type of cancer I had, the stage, or the treatment plan. On top of that, I was awaiting DNA testing results for 77 genetic conditions, including breast cancer-related syndromes. The thought of carrying a genetic risk that could impact my daughters consumed me with guilt. I was angry, too—angry at my parents for potentially passing something harmful on to me, even though I knew those thoughts weren't rational.

In therapy, we uncovered the root of my terror: the fear of having to tell my mother, a nurse in her 80s, if the tests came back positive. I could not bear the thought of making her feel the guilt and blame I was carrying. Ultimately, all that worry was unnecessary; the tests came back clear, with no genetic predispositions for any known mapped illnesses. Relief swept over me, but so did exhaustion. All that fear and energy had been spent on something that was not even real.

The most transformative advice my therapist gave me was this: *Treat yourself the way you would treat your best friend.* She pointed out that my inner critic—the "mean girl" in my head—was relentless. I had been piling on blame, guilt, and anger, with no self-compassion in sight. It was a wake-up call. I realized I would never speak to a friend the way I talked to myself.

She taught me to quiet that voice using Tara Mohr's advice: name your inner critic, picture her in an outfit, and kindly ask her to sit down rather than fight her. It was difficult, but I learned to manage the "mean girl" in my head. She is still there sometimes, but now I recognize her for what she is: a voice I don't have to listen to.

Chapter 27: Resilience-Building Practices

The practices that helped me rebuild my resilience after my accident also carried me through breast cancer treatment. These are not magic solutions, but they're tools you can develop over time to face whatever challenges come your way.

1. **Schedule Everything.** Structure gives me stability. I schedule regular dinners, lunches, and activities with friends and family. I plan my walks with my dog, Pilates classes, weight-lifting sessions, and even my downtime. For my ADHD brain, an empty calendar is a recipe for chaos, so I fill it with meaningful events. I also block time for work and adjust it as needed. Scheduling helps me take control of my time and make space for the things that matter.

2. **Move Your Body.** Resilience training emphasizes the importance of physical activity. Exercise is not just about fitness; it's also about clearing your mind, reducing stress, and feeling in control of your body. I lift weights three times a week, attend Pilates six to seven times a week, and walk my dog daily. These routines help me release frustration and sadness while grounding me in the present moment.

3. **Let Music Heal.** I learned from a personality survey that music is one of my greatest interests. I may not be a skilled singer or musician, but I enjoy attending concerts and listening to music on Spotify. Music is a constant in my life—whether it is energizing,

calming, or uplifting, it helps me process emotions and find joy.

4. **Breathe Deeply.** Breathing is a simple yet powerful tool. I use apps like Headspace to practice calming breaths and focus on breathing during Pilates. Taking time to slow down, focus on my breath, and relax helps me reduce stress and center myself. When life feels overwhelming, I take a few minutes to isolate myself and breathe deeply; I often follow this with journaling to clear my mind.

5. **Fuel Your Body.** I recently started using an app to track my calories and food intake, focusing on whole, unprocessed foods. Fruits, vegetables, and protein have become staples in my diet, and, while the scale has not moved much (thank you, Tamoxifen), I feel better and sleep more soundly. The changes may be small, but they add up to a healthier, more resilient me.

6. **Prioritize Sleep.** Sleep is non-negotiable for recovery. I aim for at least eight hours a night, though, as I have gotten older, it's become harder to sleep through the night. A cool, dark room and relaxing bedtime rituals—like reading instead of scrolling through my phone—help me rest more effectively.

7. **Limit Screen Time.** Cutting back on screen time has been a game-changer. Instead of doom-scrolling, my husband and I watch videos about hobbies we love, like travel, guitar playing, and dogs. Crawling into bed with a good book or engaging with uplifting content reduces stress and creates space for relaxation.

8. **Seek Knowledge, Not Fear.** Staying informed about my health has been empowering, but I am careful about where I get my information. I avoid Google searches that can trigger panic and instead focus on reading research papers, clinical trial results, and trusted sources. This approach helps me ask my medical team informed questions and reduces unnecessary stress.

Returning to What Grounds You

As I listened to other women's stories, I was struck by how different our sources of strength can be. Vivian leaned into her faith in God. Shelby turned toward mindfulness and self-compassion. Aurora drew on Buddhist philosophy. Erin relied on her support network. Gail focused on advocacy and physical practices. None of these paths is the same, yet all of them are valid.

For me, it's not religion. I was baptized Methodist, raised Presbyterian until age nine, and later exposed to Macumba and white-magic rituals in Brazil. I remember standing on the beach, dressed in white, placing offerings into the sea on the seventh wave after New Year's, a silky yellow belt added for luck with money. It was far from the churches I'd been raised in, yet it felt deeply meaningful—a ritual of release, hope, and renewal. Later, I married in a Catholic church and had my children baptized Catholic, allowing them to explore their faith for themselves. Over the years, I've experienced faith and ritual in many forms, and I respect them all. But when cancer shook me, I realized my own grounding came from elsewhere.

I draw strength from Humanism and Stoicism, from my family and friends, and from the conversations I have with myself—the inner dialogue that reminds me to keep moving forward. That dialogue doesn't sound like scripture or sermons; it's more like a quiet companion voice saying: *This moment is hard, but you've survived hard things before. Take one small step.*

Spirituality, for me, looks like movement and presence. Pilates has taught me to breathe, to notice where I hold tension, and to find strength even when my body feels broken. Dogs remind me of unconditional love and the healing power of play. Music carries me back to joy when I forget what it feels like. Humor interrupts fear and reminds me I am still alive. These aren't just hobbies—they're rituals. They are how I return to myself when everything else feels out of control.

The Stoics called this *memento mori*—remembering that life is finite and precious. It sounds dark, but it's actually clarifying. Knowing that time is limited pushes me to savor it, to squeeze the good out of small things. That's why I love *The Book of Awakening* by Mark Nepo. His daily reflections invite presence, gratitude, and noticing the everyday sacred, whether that's the smell of coffee, a quiet morning walk, or the sound of laughter in the next room.

Here's what I want to say clearly: whatever grounds you—faith, philosophy, ritual, or relationships—honor it. Lean into it. Don't set aside the practices that bring you comfort when cancer shakes everything loose. This is the time to return to them, to hold them close, and to let them carry you when you cannot carry yourself.

Reflection Prompt

Take a moment to think about what grounds you. Is it prayer, scripture, or meditation? Is it walking in nature, listening to music, or sharing meals with people you love? Maybe it's journaling, movement, or small daily rituals. Write them down, or return to them if they've slipped away. These are not luxuries; they are lifelines.

Moving On

Cancer is not just an individual experience; it ripples through the lives of loved ones, partners, friends, and colleagues. While undergoing treatment, I learned firsthand how much support from others could shape my journey. But I also saw how many people struggled to know what to say, how to help, or how to simply be there. In this next chapter, I share insights aimed at those who want to support someone with cancer in a truly meaningful way.

Chapter 28: Supporting Someone with Cancer

Some women tell me the most challenging part of cancer wasn't the chemo or the surgery—it was going home to an empty house afterward. If that's your reality, this section is written with you in mind. You may not have a partner or family nearby. However, there are still ways to build a network of care, find community, and maintain emotional strength.

The Power (and Weight) of Support

I am not someone who asks for help easily. My knee injury forced me to lean on others—rides to therapy, and patience from those who watched me struggle. It was uncomfortable but manageable.

However, cancer demanded more than I had ever thought I could ask for. I needed people in ways that felt unbearable. There was no "powering through." There was only surrendering to the reality that I couldn't do it alone.

When You're Going Through Breast Cancer Without a Partner or Family

Not everyone facing breast cancer has a partner, children, or family to lean on. Some of us go through treatment while living alone, raising ourselves up each day without a built-in safety net. If that's you, I want to say this clearly: you are not less worthy of care, support, or compassion. Your strength is not measured by whether someone is waiting at home for you.

Here are some ways to help yourself feel supported, even if family isn't nearby:

1. **Build your chosen circle.** Think of friends, colleagues, neighbors, or community members as your extended healthcare team: one could drive you to treatment, another could check in by text, and someone else could drop off a meal. Sometimes people want to help but don't know how. Make a short list of tasks you'd welcome, and share it when they ask.

2. **Use the support systems around you.** Most cancer centers have social workers, patient navigators, or volunteers who can connect you with resources such as rides, meal delivery, or financial assistance. They don't have to do everything—one person might handle meals, another might help with transportation, and someone else might simply check in with you by text. Organizations like Gilda's Club, Cancer Support Community, and hospital-based support groups exist for people exactly like you—those who don't want to walk this road alone.

3. **Consider professional help.** If it's within your means, think about hiring help for the practical stuff—grocery delivery, pet care, house cleaning— especially during chemo or surgery recovery. This isn't indulgent; it's survival.

4. **Take care of your emotional health.** Journaling, voice notes, art, or prayer can become companions when you don't have a partner to talk to at the end of the day. Online groups are also powerful— thousands of women connect daily in private forums, sharing tips, venting, and celebrating small victories together.

5. **Plan ahead for treatment days.** If anesthesia or sedation is involved, most hospitals require someone to sign you out. Ask a friend, a neighbor, or even a faith community member to be your "on-call" person. Some treatment centers also provide volunteer companions for this very reason—don't hesitate to ask.

6. **Remember: you belong.** Being single, child-free, widowed, divorced, or far from family doesn't make your journey less valid. Your resilience is real. You deserve the same compassion, patience, and care as anyone else.

Going through cancer without a partner or family may feel daunting, but it does not make you less whole, less loved, or less capable. The truth is, resilience often grows in unexpected places—through friendships, community, and even within your own quiet strength. You are not defined by who stands beside you, but by how you choose to keep standing. Whatever your circumstances, you deserve compassion, dignity, and support.

Chapter 29: Understanding the Circle of Support

A cancer diagnosis ripples outward, touching not just the person at the center but also their loved ones, coworkers, and friends. Everyone wants to help, but not everyone plays the same role. Some people are directly involved in daily care, while others provide support from a distance. The Circle of Support, also known as "Ring Theory," was first described by Susan Silk and Barry Goldman in the Los Angeles Times (2013). They summed it up with the Golden Rule: *comfort in, dump out.* I've adapted their idea here for the breast cancer journey because it so clearly explains how support should flow.

One helpful way to think about the relationships among those involved is to visualize concentric circles showing who is closest to the patient and how care and communication flow among them.

The person with cancer is at the center.

Their closest family and caregivers form the next circle.

Friends, extended family, and colleagues make up the outermost circle.

The guiding principle is simple:

Support flows INWARD—offer encouragement, practical help, and a listening ear to those closer to the center.

Venting flows OUTWARD—process your fears, stress, or grief with people in larger circles, not with those closer to the crisis.

Circle of Support: Comfort In, Dump Out

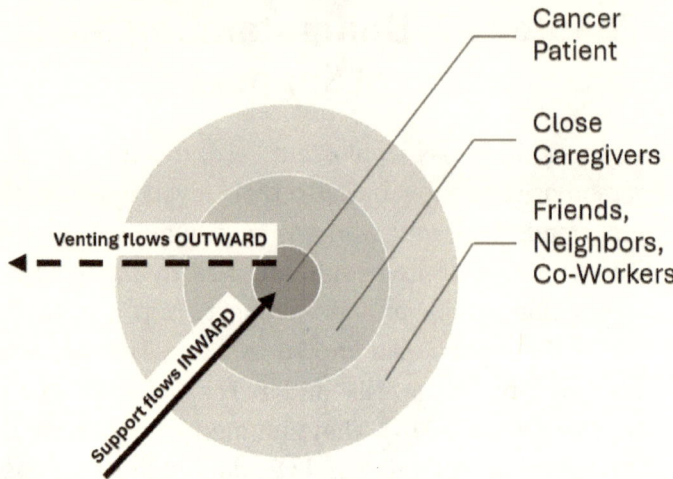

Example: If you're a friend of the patient's spouse, don't tell the patient how hard this is for you—offer them support instead. Share your feelings with someone further out in the circles.

Cancer Impacts Families, Too

Cancer doesn't just happen to an individual—it happens to an entire family.

- Spouses, children, parents, and siblings all experience their own grief, fear, and uncertainty.

- While their pain is different from the patient's, it is real.

- Acknowledging their struggles—without placing the burden of comfort on the patient—makes a huge difference.

Offering support means more than just saying the right thing; it's about truly listening and making space for the reality of what someone is going through.

The Golden Rule: Comfort In, Dumping Out

Just to emphasize this point, if you're feeling overwhelmed, **don't share that with the patient**—lean on those further out in the circle. Encouragement and support should always be directed toward the person most affected to strengthen them.

Example: A co-worker who wants to help should reach out to the patient's close friend or family member first, rather than directly sharing their concerns or emotions with the patient.

Close Support: The Middle Circle (Partners, Family, and Immediate Friends)

If you are in the **middle circle**, you are probably a primary caregiver or deeply involved in the patient's life. That means you may also experience stress, grief, and exhaustion. You must find your own sources of support so that you don't place an additional burden on the patient.

How to Be a Meaningful Supporter: Living with a Cancer Patient

Living with someone undergoing cancer treatment is challenging, but your role is vital. Here are a few ways to offer meaningful support:

- **Release the Patient from Expectations:** Their primary job is to get through the treatment. Reassure them that it's okay if they can't handle household responsibilities. Celebrate small victories—like when they feel up to making a meal or helping around the house—but never expect them to perform. Gratitude and patience go a long way.

- **Work Together on Essentials:** Being fed, hydrated, and kept clean can feel monumental during treatment. Share these responsibilities or step in when they cannot. Encourage a rhythm that prioritizes their comfort and well-being.

- **Be Present Without Intruding:** Some patients, like me, prefer solitude during chemo. Respect their preferences and offer support in ways they find helpful—whether that's a quiet ride to appointments or waiting outside until they're ready to talk.

Checking Your Own Issues before Offering Support

When someone you care about is battling cancer, it's natural to want to help—but make sure your actions genuinely serve their needs. Here's how to self-reflect before stepping in:

- **Avoid Toxic Positivity:** Saying things like, "Everything happens for a reason" or "At least it's not worse" might come from a good place, but it can feel dismissive. Instead, acknowledge their experience: *"This must be so hard. I am here for you."*

- **Offer Practical Support:** Tangible help—like driving them to appointments, cooking meals, or managing errands—is far more meaningful than vague offers like, "Let me know if you need anything."

- **Recognize Your Own Emotions:** If seeing your loved one when they are sick brings up feelings of sadness, fear, or helplessness, process those emotions elsewhere. Lean on your circle for venting and comfort so that you can be there for the patient.

When Well-Meaning Comments Hurt

After treatment, I struggled with the way that people reacted to my appearance. Many commented on how great my hair looked as it grew back. I know they meant well, but I hated my new hair. It was short, curly, and nothing like the long, flowing hair I had cherished.

It felt like they preferred post-cancer me to pre-cancer me, as if the person I was before had somehow been erased. I was mourning the old me—my identity tied to that version of myself—and their insistence that my new hair was "great" invalidated my grief.

Tip: To anyone supporting a loved one through changes like this, remember: Sometimes, the best thing you can do is acknowledge their feelings without trying to fix or reframe them. A simple *"I hear you"* or *"I'm sorry you're feeling this way"* can mean the world.

Distant Support: The Outer Circle (Friends, Neighbors, and Co-Workers)

If you're in the **outer circle**, your job is to provide **help, not burdens.** Avoid venting your fears to the patient or their close caregivers—offer encouragement, practical support, and respect boundaries. Caregivers in the middle circle:

consider providing this information to members of your loved ones' Outer Circle.

1. Offer Normality

Cancer doesn't change who a person is. Continue to invite them to lunches, dinners, and outings when they feel up to it. Even if they decline, the act of reaching out shows that you care. Avoid treating them differently or tiptoeing around their diagnosis unless they express discomfort. Sometimes, the greatest comfort is being treated like a friend, not a patient.

2. Be Specific in Your Offers of Help

Vague offers like *"Let me know if you need anything"* can feel overwhelming for someone navigating treatment. Instead, make clear, actionable offers:

- "I'm heading to the pharmacy—can I pick up anything for you?"

- "I'm swinging by the grocery store—what can I grab for you?"

- "I will be in your area this afternoon. Can I quickly visit and take out your trash or help with errands?"

By being specific, you reduce the mental load on the person you are supporting and make it easier for them to accept your help.

3. Respect Boundaries

Some days, they may crave connection, while on other days, they may need space to rest and recover. Honor their preferences without taking their responses personally.

If you drop off a meal or supplies, text or ring the bell, and support them without the pressure of social interaction, they might not be up for it.

4. Lighten Their Load

Consider taking on small, everyday tasks that may feel monumental during treatment. Offer to:

- Take out their trash or recycling.
- Walk their dog or water their plants.
- Drop off pre-cooked meals or snacks that require minimal preparation.
- Help coordinate rides to appointments or schedule reminders for important dates.

These practical contributions can make a huge difference in their day-to-day life.

5. Check in, but Do Not Hover

Regular check-ins, like a quick text or a thoughtful card, show you are thinking of them without being intrusive. Avoid constant updates or pressure to keep the conversation going, and let them set the pace of communication.

A simple *"Thinking of you today"* or *"No need to reply, just wanted to say hi"* can brighten their day.

6. Avoid Toxic Positivity

As we've seen, phrases like *"You're so strong"* or *"Everything happens for a reason"* may feel dismissive of their real struggles. Instead, acknowledge their feelings and offer empathy. Say things like:

- *"This sounds so hard. I am here if you need me."*

- *"I can't imagine what you're going through, but I want to help however I can."*

Authentic compassion means far more than empty platitudes.

7. Normalize the Relationship

One of the greatest gifts you can give is treating them as the same person they have always been. Share updates about your life, tell them funny stories, or chat about topics unrelated to cancer. Normality is a powerful way to remind them that they are more than their diagnosis.

Using the Circle of Support to Show Up in the Best Way

When supporting someone with cancer, it's essential to understand where you fit in their circle of support. If you're close, be there emotionally and seek your own support elsewhere. If you're further out, your role is to ease the patient's burden, not add to it.

Cancer is hard enough; let's ensure we're showing up in ways that genuinely help.

Chapter 30: Coping with Hair Loss

Before cancer, my hair hung down my back, long and thick. My bangs framed my face, softening one of my biggest insecurities, my nearly invisible eyebrows. I had stopped dyeing it years before, so I was already used to the gray. But when my hair started growing back during chemo, the gray came in first—strong, stubborn, and wiry—while the darker hairs took much longer to return. It felt like my body had aged faster than my mind.

People were eager to reassure me. "I love your curls!" they would say. "It suits you so well!" I knew they meant well, but it didn't feel like a compliment. My short, curly hair wasn't me. It was a constant reminder of what cancer had taken away. My missing bangs made my light eyebrows stand out even more, amplifying my insecurity. My new hair wasn't a return to normal—it was evidence of how much had changed.

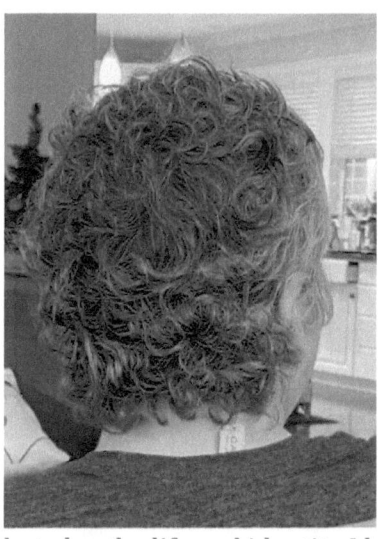

I longed for my old hair, the hair that had felt like **me**. Hearing others celebrate this new look, even with the best intentions, left me feeling unseen. It was as though they preferred the "post-cancer" version of me to the person I had been before. It added to the grief I already felt, mourning not just my body's changes but also the life and identity I had before my diagnosis.

I knew the comments people made came from a place of kindness. People were trying to help, to find something positive in the middle of so much loss. I am not angry with them, and I never was. But those well-intentioned words didn't land the way they hoped. Instead, they reminded me of the gap between how I felt inside and how others perceived me.

Tips For Caregivers

When someone is going through cancer, well-intentioned words and actions don't always land as expected. Instead of focusing on what you think might be comforting, ask open-ended questions that give them space to express their needs.

DO: Ask open-ended questions instead of making assumptions.

"How are you feeling about all the changes?"

"Is there anything you miss or are still getting used to?"

"What can I do to support you right now?"

DON'T: Use dismissive or toxic positivity phrases.

"You're so strong!" (This can feel like pressure, not comfort.)

"At least you're alive!" (Minimizing someone's struggle doesn't help.)

"Your hair looks great!" (Even if this is true, it can feel invalidating.)

Chapter 31: Avoiding Toxic Positivity

When someone you love is diagnosed with cancer, it's human to feel helpless. You want to say the right thing. You want to lift their spirits. You want them to know you believe they'll get through it.

You mean well. However, sometimes, good intentions land like glitter on a gaping wound.

What Is Toxic Positivity?

Toxic positivity is the urge to "just think positive" even when the person in front of you is drowning in fear or grief. It's when your need to offer hope overrides their need to be honest. You may mean well, but harm still happens. In the moment, it can sound like encouragement. Underneath, it often says: "Your pain makes me uncomfortable. Please hide it for me."

Let's be clear: optimism isn't the enemy. Forced cheerfulness is.

What Toxic Positivity Sounds Like

You've probably heard—or maybe even said—some of these:

- "Stay positive!"
- "You've got this, you're so strong."
- "Everything happens for a reason."
- "At least it's not worse."
- "God only gives you what you can handle."
- "Just keep fighting. I knew someone who beat it!"

These might feel supportive to say. When you're on the receiving end, it can feel like someone has walked right past your pain, tossed a motivational quote over their shoulder, and called it love. Even "strength" comments can backfire. What if they are not feeling strong? Do you want them to feel guilty for not living up to your expectations of their strength?

Why It Hurts More Than It Helps

"I told my friend I was scared, and she said, 'Don't be!' — like it was that simple. I shut down. I never brought it up again."

Toxic positivity isn't comforting. It's minimizing. It sends the message that there's only one acceptable version of you: the strong one, the hopeful one, the one who's already fine. Everything else—your fear, your grief, your rage—gets quietly swept aside.

When someone responds with forced optimism, it doesn't feel like love. It feels like:

- My pain makes you uncomfortable.

- I have to look, act, and speak strongly just to make *you* feel okay.

- There's no room for honesty.

- I've failed because I'm scared.

- You care more about your comfort than my reality.

In trying to help, you may be unintentionally asking someone to hide the truth of what they're living through.

It's not that hope is harmful. It's that enforced hope is.

Toxic positivity:

- Shuts down grief, anger, and fear.

- Centers on the speaker's discomfort rather than the patient's experience.

- Pressures the patient to "perform" emotional resilience.

- Sends the message: *Your real emotions aren't welcome here.*

Gut Check: Are You Centering Them or Yourself?

If someone shared their scariest truth with you, would they feel heard—or hurried toward hope?

Ask yourself:

- Am I trying to make *them* feel better—or *am I trying to make myself feel better*?

- Did I just say "at least"?

- Am I glossing over something hard because it's uncomfortable?

- Did I just hand them a silver lining they didn't ask for?

This isn't about blame. It's about awareness. Awareness is the first step toward real support.

What to Say Instead

Support doesn't need to be polished. It just needs to be real.

Try this:

- "That sounds awful. I'm so sorry you're going through this."

- "You don't have to be positive for me."

- "I'm here to listen—even if it's messy."

- "What do you wish people would stop saying to you?"

- "I don't know what to say except I love you. I'm here."

I had friends who specifically said or texted me a few of these. They helped me feel seen, heard, and supported.

What if you've said the wrong thing? Try: "I'm sorry. I was trying to help, and I missed it. Thanks for telling me."

Then stop. Don't defend. Don't explain. Just show up better next time.

What Actually Helps

Things you can *do*:

- Drop off a meal and don't linger.
- Send a text: "Thinking of you—no need to reply."
- Venmo some cash so they can order takeout.
- Clean something when you visit—quietly.
    - Send a meme if that's your love language.
    - Let them cry. Let them rage. Let them go quiet. Let them not feel strong.

Performative Support vs. Real Support

There's a kind of support that looks like support but doesn't *feel* like it. You'll know it when you see it. It's the pink-ribbon posts with no follow-up text. It's the "my friend has cancer" whisper dropped into conversation for a little borrowed sadness or borrowed credibility. It's walking a 5K in her honor, and never sending a text to see how she's doing. It's glitter on a gaping wound.

That's not support.

Don't tag me in your photo from the breast cancer walk if you never showed up when I needed childcare or a meal. Don't tell your network how brave I am if you never asked what scared me. Don't post pink in October and disappear the rest of the year.

It's not that public support is bad—awareness matters. Fundraisers matter. When you use someone's suffering to look good or feel better about yourself without actually offering meaningful help, that's performative. And it stings. It turns our very real pain into a marketing campaign you never got consent to run.

If you want to help, don't make it about you. Ask how they want to be supported. Honor their boundaries. Offer something tangible. And do it without needing praise or credit. Quiet care is always more powerful than loud performance.

Sometimes the most loving thing you can do is stay silent. Let them lead. Let them say no. Let them *own their story.*

When Support Becomes Spotlight-Stealing

Maybe you've heard the term "virtue signaling" before and are now wondering what it looks like in the cancer world?

It's the friend who shaves her head "in solidarity"—and posts it all over Facebook, tagging you without asking. It's the neighbor who brags about being there for you... without actually asking what you need.

It's performative support. It's centering yourself in someone else's suffering. It's doing something "kind" in a way that still grabs the spotlight.

Let's say it clearly: **You don't get to hijack someone else's illness to make yourself look generous or woke or brave.**

Especially not when they're still trying to survive.

One woman told me, "Every time I saw my friend's bald head that she shaved in 'solidarity,' it reminded me that *I* was sick. That I didn't choose this. That I had lost control. Her gesture wasn't comforting—it was a mirror I never asked for."

Virtue signaling isn't about showing up. It's about being *seen while showing up.*

Don't Share Their Story Without Consent

Losing your hair, your breasts, your energy, your ability to plan—that's already more than enough loss. But when someone shares your diagnosis without your permission? That strips away one of the last things you still have: control of your own story.

And it happens all the time. A neighbor casually drops it at the book club. A colleague tells your work friend, "Just so they know." A family member posts a vague "prayers up" message and reveals everything. Suddenly, you're the topic of conversations you never agreed to.

It may seem harmless, even well-meaning. It's not. It's invasive. It's a form of social theft. And it's devastating.

After my diagnosis, I kept my circle small—on purpose. I wasn't ready for the tidal wave of sympathy, the constant check-ins, the well-meaning yet exhausting messages. I needed time to understand the language of my disease, the plan, the odds. I needed space to rage and grieve. And I needed control.

The people I told early got it. They didn't post. They didn't whisper. They let me fall apart safely.

Not everyone gets that grace. I've seen so many women whose stories were shared before they had even met with an oncologist. Before they had decided how to tell their children. Before they could say, "Yes, this is my reality—and here's how I want to share it."

Once it's out there, you can't get it back.

Don't take away someone's power to choose how they're introduced to the world as a cancer patient. Let them decide if, when, and how to share.

If You're Not Sure—Say Nothing

If you're not sure? Don't hint. Don't post. Don't share. If you wouldn't want someone live-blogging your worst medical moment, don't do it to them. If it's not your diagnosis, it's not your story to tell.

Not every ache needs a pep talk.

If you're not sure what to say—say nothing. Silence, when offered with care, can be a gift. A quiet presence says: *I'm here. I can hold this with you.*

That's infinitely better than blurting out a chipper *"You got this!"* Let the moment breathe. Let it be what it is.

You Don't Have to Fix It

Here's the truth: You can't fix this. You can't cheer it away.

You can't explain it, fast-forward it, or wrap it up in platitudes.

You *can* make it less lonely.

You do that by showing up without a script.

By letting the person you love cry, rage, or shut down—and staying beside them anyway.

By holding space for their fear without trying to convert it into hope before they're ready.

You don't need magic words. You need presence. Steady, unflinching presence.

Preventing A Toxically Positive Response

Ask yourself:

1. Am I offering comfort—or trying to fix it?

2. Am I making space—or filling it with noise?

3. Am I supporting them—or soothing my own discomfort?

Still not sure? Then wait. Breathe. Listen. Let them lead the conversation. That's how you love someone through this.

And if you've said the wrong thing before? Don't retreat. Don't disappear in embarrassment. Apologize. Own it. Show up again—better this time.

Because what matters most... is that you come back and you support them throughout their journey.

Moving On

Cancer doesn't live in a vacuum. While patients and families are the ones in the exam rooms and infusion chairs, the ripple effect reaches far beyond—to workplaces, teams, and managers. Many of us don't have the option to step away from work entirely, and even when we do, the return can be daunting.

Section Five shifts the lens outward. It's about how workplaces can support employees who are facing cancer, caregiving, or recovery—and why compassion at work matters for everyone. This section is written not just for managers but for organizations that want to do better by their people when life shows up at the office door. For downloadable manager checklists and workplace guides, visit: **vikkiespinosawrites.com/pages/resources.**

SECTION FIVE

A Guide for Workplaces and Managers

Most of us don't get to leave work behind when cancer enters our lives. Even when our bodies are in infusion chairs or exam rooms, a big part of our lives still lives at work. That's why compassion in the workplace matters—whether you're a manager, a teammate, or an organization. This section provides practical guidance on supporting individuals through treatment, caregiving, and their return to work.

Chapter 32: Why Support Matters at Work

No one gets through their entire career — potentially 30 to 40 years — without needing support.

At some point, every employee (including leaders) will face a health crisis, a family emergency, or another major challenge. Great workplaces understand that business is about people. How a company supports employees through challenging times shapes culture, engagement, and long-term loyalty.

- Supporting one employee well sends a powerful message to everyone watching.

- A culture of care leads to higher retention, morale, and trust.

- Employees who feel supported are more likely to return engaged and motivated.

Supporting Employees with Cancer: A Workplace Guide

When an employee receives a cancer diagnosis, the impact extends beyond their personal life—it affects their work life, their team, and the overall organization. Many employees continue working through treatment, balancing medical appointments, fatigue, and side effects with their job responsibilities. Others may require extended leave and a supportive transition back to work upon completing treatment.

As a manager or company leader, your response can either alleviate or compound an employee's stress. Your goal is to create a culture where employees feel supported, valued, and empowered to prioritize their health, without sacrificing job stability.

Here's how to build that culture.

Six Core Actions for Managers

Step 1: Have a Private, Compassionate Conversation

- Listen without judgment. Let them share as much or as little as they want.

- Ask about their needs. Avoid assumptions. Instead ask:
    - "How can we best support you at work?"
    - "What adjustments would be helpful during treatment?"

- Protect their privacy. Do not share their news without permission.

What to Say Instead of "You've Got This": "I know this must be difficult. You have my full support. We'll work through this together."

Step 2: Reassure with Job Security and Flexibility

Many employees battling cancer feel guilty for missing work or fear being seen as unreliable. Treatment is unpredictable—some days they'll feel well enough to work, others they won't. Your job is to reduce their fear and guilt and to show flexibility.

What Managers Can Say to Alleviate Anxiety:

- "Your health comes first. We will adjust your workload as needed."

- "You're a valued part of this team, and your job is secure while you focus on your recovery."

- "We'll work together on a plan that makes sense for you."

Best Practices During Treatment:

- Offer flexible scheduling—half-days, shifted hours, or a hybrid model.

- Enable remote work if their role allows.

- Avoid assigning high-stakes projects or expecting the same performance as before diagnosis.

- Respect their preferences; some may want to work through treatment, while others may need full-time off.

Share available resources proactively: Disability leave, FMLA (U.S. Department of Labor, 2023), or employee assistance programs (EAPs) are often unknown until someone asks. Don't make them ask.

Step 3: Know the Legal Protections

As a manager, you don't have to be an expert, but you do need to understand the basics of workplace protections.

Key Laws That May Apply:

- **FMLA (Family and Medical Leave Act):** Provides up to 12 weeks of unpaid leave with job protection (U.S. Department of Labor, 2023).

- **ADA (Americans with Disabilities Act):** Requires reasonable accommodations for medical conditions, including cancer (U.S. Equal Employment Opportunity Commission, n.d.).

- **Short- and Long-Term Disability:** These employer-sponsored benefits can provide partial income during extended leave. Check your handbook or website for guidance, and be sure to share the information with your employees.

Tip: Partner with HR to ensure the employee receives accurate information early and doesn't feel abandoned.

Note: These laws apply in the U.S. If you're outside the U.S., check your country's workplace protections and employee rights.

Step 4: Support Employees Who Are Caregivers

Cancer impacts whole families. Caregivers may be just as overwhelmed, exhausted, and emotionally spent as the person diagnosed. Your support matters here, too.

I saw this firsthand with one of my employees. His mother was undergoing breast cancer treatment. Balancing work, doctor visits, and stress was draining him. I offered flexibility and understanding. Later, he told me how much it meant to be able to support his mom without risking his job. That's leadership.

How to Support Caregivers:

- Offer schedule flexibility—caregivers may need to attend appointments or take calls.

- Enable remote work where feasible.

- Normalize mental health days and emotional check-ins.

- Share EAP and mental health resources.

- Acknowledge the emotional burden, not just the logistics.

Caregivers often need the same compassion and flexibility as patients.

Step 5: Help with the Return to Work

Coming back after cancer treatment isn't a switch; it's a slow re-entry. Side effects like fatigue, "chemo brain," or physical limitations can linger.

How to Make Reintegration Smoother:

- Allow for a gradual return—part-time hours at first, if possible.

- Reset expectations around performance and timelines.

- Offer flexible breaks and accommodations.

- Provide ergonomic tools or seating, if needed.

Assign a "work buddy" to support social reintegration and reduce isolation.

Returning to work can be healing—but only if the environment is safe, patient, and realistic.

Chapter 33: Leading Through Crisis: The Culture Test

A major health crisis isn't just a challenge for the person diagnosed—it's a test of your company's values.

Would your team feel safe disclosing a cancer diagnosis? Would they expect to be supported, or fear being judged or pushed out?

Great leaders don't just manage—they model the culture they want.

Leadership Insight: How you treat employees in crisis defines your workplace far more than any mission statement or employee perk ever will.

Replace PTO Donation with Real Support

One common but problematic practice? Asking coworkers to donate paid time off to help a peer with cancer. It seems generous, but it quietly shifts the employer's responsibility onto employees. If your company already has a donation program, here's how to improve it.

The Problems with PTO Donation:

- Creates pressure to give up personal time.
- Exacerbates inequity (higher earners can afford to donate; others can't).
- Sends the message that the company won't step in unless coworkers do.

What to Do Instead:

- Create a **company-funded** medical leave pool.
- Offer extended paid leave options for serious health events.

- Communicate leave options clearly and early.

The Business Case for Supporting Employees

Some leaders focus only on the short-term costs of leave or accommodations. But the return on investment (ROI) is tangible and measurable.

Why It's Smart Business:

- **Retention**: Employees supported during a crisis are more loyal and more likely to stay.
- **Reputation**: People talk. Companies known for treating people well attract better talent.
- **Engagement**: Employees who feel valued come back stronger, more committed, and more productive.

Gallup research shows that employees who strongly agree their employer cares about their overall well-being are 69% less likely to be actively looking for a new job. (Harter, 2023)

Great workplaces invest in people, and they get better performance in return.

Build a Culture That Puts People First

A cancer diagnosis affects more than one person. It touches teams, families, and your broader culture. Leaders can normalize support—without prying or overstepping—by making it clear that health challenges are not career-ending events.

How Leadership Creates a Supportive Culture:

- **Respect privacy**—Never share unless given permission.
- **Check in**—Genuine questions like, "What would help this week?" go a long way.

- **Avoid comparisons**—Don't say, "My cousin had the same thing."

Not everyone wants to talk about their cancer, but they do want to feel safe and seen.

Invest in Training, Policies, and Perspective

Many managers feel unprepared to respond well when someone discloses a diagnosis. That's solvable.

What Employers Can Offer:

- Training in compassionate and professional communication.
- Clear HR policies around accommodations and leave.
- Resources on ADA, FMLA, and relevant state laws.
- Partnerships with cancer organizations for education and support.

Don't Forget Younger Employees

Supporting employees through cancer isn't just about policies and benefits—it's about creating a culture of humanity. That culture runs through this entire book: at home, in friendships, and at work, the way we show up for each other matters.

Breast cancer is increasingly being diagnosed in women in their 20s and 30s, early-career professionals facing different barriers.

Unique Challenges:

- **Fertility impacts**—treatment may affect reproductive options.
- **Financial stress**—limited savings and early-career salaries.

- **Career disruption**—concerns about long-term trajectory.

Best Practices:

- Offer fertility guidance and preservation resources.
- Provide clear communication on job stability.
- Normalize flexible paths for returning to work or adjusting responsibilities.

In the End: Will Your Workplace Rise to the Moment?

A culture of care doesn't just help people survive cancer—it helps them thrive after. The best workplaces don't wait for a crisis to build support. They start now. Supporting employees through cancer isn't just about policies and benefits—it's about creating a culture of humanity. That culture is the thread that runs through this entire book: whether in our homes, our friendships, or our workplaces, the way we show up for each other matters.

Moving On

We've walked through the story, the reflections, the voices of others, and the practical guidance. To close, I've gathered the resources I leaned on—and the ones I wish I'd known about sooner.

Section Six is meant to be picked up and used: checklists, practical tips, recommended books and support groups, and tools to help you or someone you care about. Whether you're preparing for treatment, walking alongside a friend, or leading a team at work, this section gives you concrete ways to take action.

SECTION SIX

Resources, Checklists & Practical Tools

Sometimes you don't want a story—you just need a list. This section is a grab-and-go collection of resources, checklists, and practical guides for patients, caregivers, and workplaces. Use it however it serves you best.

Chapter 34: Getting Ready

When undergoing cancer treatment, even small tasks can feel overwhelming. Preparing ahead of time can **reduce stress, conserve energy, and ensure you have what you need** within easy reach. These comprehensive lists will help you get ready.

Printable versions of the lists and other resources are available on my website.

vikkiespinosawrites.com/pages/resources

Stock Up on Essentials: Home & Daily Life

Food and Meal Prep
- Stock your fridge and freezer with ready-to-eat meals, soups, and easy snacks.
- Ask a friend or family member to coordinate a meal train so that meals arrive on a schedule that suits you. (Tip: Don't get food every day; you'll probably have leftovers and need variety.)
- Prepare small portions of high-protein foods (for example, Greek yogurt, cottage cheese, eggs, chicken, tofu, smoothies).
- Have bland foods on hand in case of nausea (crackers, toast, applesauce, plain rice, bananas).
- Buy protein shakes, in case eating solid food is difficult.
- Order grocery delivery or set up a shopping routine with a friend or family member.

Household Items
- Stock up on toilet paper, tissues, paper towels, cleaning wipes, and hand sanitizer.
- Buy fragrance-free detergent and gentle soaps; strong scents may trigger nausea.

- Keep unscented lotion, lip balm, and gentle skincare handy (chemo can dry out your skin).
- Use a non-alcoholic mouthwash to help prevent mouth sores.
- Keep a thermometer to check for fever (chemo weakens the immune system).
- Buy a pill organizer; your brain will be foggy, and keeping track of medications will be hard.
- Have small plastic or disposable vomit bags near your bed, in the car, and in your chemo bag.
- Consider if your chemo medication is known to affect bowel control, and whether you might need incontinence pads.

Hydration and Comfort

- Stock up on hydration drinks (like Gatorade Zero, Pedialyte, electrolyte powders, and coconut water).
- Keep a large water bottle with a straw nearby at all times.
- Get a humidifier if dry mouth or dry skin becomes a problem.
- Have peppermint tea or ginger chews for nausea.

Create a Rest and Recovery Space

Bedroom Setup

- Arrange a cozy, quiet space for resting: your bed or a comfortable recliner with plenty of pillows and blankets.
- Keep a small table or nightstand next to your resting spot for medications, water, snacks, and a notebook.
- Have a weighted blanket if anxiety or body pain makes sleeping difficult.
- Use soft sheets and a silk pillowcase; your skin may become extra sensitive.
- Get a wedge pillow to help with acid reflux or nausea.

Bathroom Adjustments

- Install a shower chair; standing up for long showers can be exhausting.
- Get non-slip bath mats to prevent falls if you feel weak.
- Keep baby wipes or unscented cleansing wipes nearby for quick freshening up.
- Use a gentle or all-natural deodorant; some deodorants may irritate sensitive skin.
- If radiation treatment is planned, buy a strong hydrocortisone cream to prevent or treat skin irritation.
- Have small baskets in key areas (bedroom, couch, and bathroom) with essentials like tissues, lip balm, and hand lotion.

Household Chores and Help

Ask for Support

- Accept help with cleaning; you will not have the energy to vacuum, scrub, or mop.
- Hire a house cleaner (or have a friend organize a cleaning crew) to do light housekeeping. Some non-profits offer this service.
- Ask a neighbor or friend to take out your trash cans; this takes more energy than you think.
- Plan for pet care. Who will walk your dog, feed the cat, or take care of the litter boxes when you can't leave the house?
- Set up a laundry plan; ask for help with washing, drying, and putting away clothes.
- Declutter common areas to reduce tripping hazards when you feel weak or lightheaded.

Tech and Entertainment

- Download movies, TV shows, audiobooks, and podcasts to keep yourself entertained during long rest periods.
- Create a music playlist for relaxation or motivation.

- Have headphones (preferably noise-canceling) to drown out background noise.
- Set up a tablet or laptop near your resting spot for easy browsing.
- Use a digital calendar to track medical appointments, medications, and side effects.

Transportation and Planning

Arrange Rides and Support

- Do not drive yourself to chemo; you may be too fatigued or dizzy afterward.
- Set up a ride schedule with friends, family, or a ride service. Nonprofits and volunteers also provide this service.
- Keep a small vomit bag in the car in case of nausea.
- Consider wearing adult diapers for longer car rides if bowel control becomes unpredictable.
- If possible, plan for a flexible work schedule or leave of absence; even part-time hours may be exhausting.

Final Tips: Give Yourself Grace

You do not have to do everything alone. Cancer treatment will take up much of your physical and mental energy, so let people help, even if it is just taking out the trash or running an errand for you. Accepting help is a strength, not a weakness.

Some days will be harder than others. If you do not get everything on your list, that is okay. Focus on what helps you feel comfortable and cared for. Prepare for the unexpected. Side effects and energy levels will fluctuate. Having a plan in place makes life easier when those tough days hit.

Chapter 35: Questions and Planning Lists for Treatment and Beyond

When you are facing cancer treatment, the sheer amount of information, appointments, and decisions can feel overwhelming. You are suddenly managing a schedule filled with blood tests, scans, and infusions, all while trying to keep your home running and your body as strong as possible. If you are anything like me, you want clear, actionable steps, things you can do to prepare, and ways others can help without having to guess what you need.

That is where the lists below come in. They are the lists I wish I had had before I started treatment. They cover what to ask, what to prepare at home, what to bring to chemo, and what to expect afterward. Some of these lessons I learned the hard way, like realizing how much energy it takes to take out the trash or how bone pain from chemo could have been eased with Claritin. Others come from the wisdom of fellow patients who have already walked this road.

You do not have to do everything at once, and you certainly do not have to do it alone. But you can use these lists as a guide to taking control of what you can and setting yourself up for the best possible experience. And if someone asks, "How can I help?" hand them a list. They will be grateful for the direction, and you will be thankful for the support.

Questions to Ask Your Doctor

When you are newly diagnosed, it can feel impossible to know what to ask or even where to start. I remember sitting in appointments, my mind spinning so fast I could not hold on to a single thought once the doctor started talking. That is normal. Cancer brings information overload.

This list is meant to be a practical tool, not a script you have to follow word-for-word. Take the questions that matter to you, skip the rest, and add your own. You may even want to bring a friend or partner to take notes so you can focus on listening.

Keep in mind: your doctors expect questions. Asking them does not make you difficult; it makes you an active participant in your care.

Diagnosis and Treatment

- What type of breast cancer do I have (ER-positive, HER2-positive, triple-negative, or one of the less common types)?
- What stage is my cancer, and what does that mean for treatment?
- Has my cancer spread to my lymph nodes or anywhere else?
- What are my treatment options, and which do you recommend?
- What are the goals of this treatment?
- What are the risks if I choose to delay or refuse treatment?
- How do we know if this treatment is working?
- Are there any clinical trials I should consider?

Surgery and Reconstruction

- Do I need a lumpectomy or mastectomy?
- What are my breast reconstruction options?
- If I do not do reconstruction now, what are my other options (prosthetics, surgery later, something else)?
- How long is the recovery period after surgery?
- Will I need physical therapy afterward?
- What should I do to prepare for surgery?
- What are the risks of developing lymphedema after surgery, and how can I reduce them?

Chemotherapy and Radiation

- What type of chemo will I receive, and how does it work?
- How long will chemo take, and how often will I need treatments?
- What side effects should I expect from chemotherapy?
- Are there medications to help with nausea and fatigue?
- Should I use cold caps to try to keep my hair?
- What should I expect from radiation therapy?
- Will radiation increase my risk of lymphedema?
- How long do radiation side effects last?
- How can I prepare for chemo and radiation treatment?

Hormone Therapy and Medications

- Will I need hormone therapy (Tamoxifen, aromatase inhibitors, something else)?
- What are the long-term side effects of hormone therapy?
- If I am premenopausal, will this treatment push me into early menopause?
- How will treatment affect my bone health?
- Are there any supplements or medications I should avoid?
- Will hormone therapy impact my ability to lose or maintain weight?
- What are the risks of taking HRT (hormone replacement therapy) after treatment?

Fertility and Sexual Health

- Will chemo or hormone therapy affect my fertility?
- Can I freeze my eggs before starting treatment?
- What are the risks of pregnancy after breast cancer treatment?
- How will treatment affect my sex drive or vaginal health?
- Are there safe options for managing menopause symptoms?
- Will my insurance cover fertility preservation?

- Are there resources that deal with sexual health and intimacy after cancer treatment?

Daily Life and Managing Side Effects

- How will treatment affect my energy levels and ability to work?
- What foods should I eat or avoid during treatment?
- Will I need to change my exercise routine?
- How do I manage chemo brain or memory issues?
- What can I do to relieve joint pain and muscle stiffness?
- How can I reduce my risk of infections during chemo?
- What over-the-counter medications should I avoid during treatment?
- What should I do if I experience new or worsening symptoms?
- What happens if I need to miss a treatment session?
- Are there alternative or complementary therapies that can help manage symptoms?

Long-Term Health and Recurrence Risk

- What are the chances of my cancer coming back?
- What can I do to lower my risk of recurrence?
- How often will I need follow-up scans or bloodwork?
- If my cancer returns, what are the next steps?
- Will I need genetic testing to see if my family is at higher risk?
- Should my family members get genetic testing for BRCA or other mutations?
- What lifestyle changes can help my recovery and reduce my risk?
- Are there support groups or counseling options available?

Plan Ahead for Chemo: Before, During, After

Preparing for chemotherapy involves more than just showing up for your infusion. Your body, mind, and home all need preparation to help manage side effects and reduce stress. Here is a comprehensive guide to get ready for your first chemo session.

Schedule and Logistics

Understand the Treatment Plan

- Ask your doctor for a detailed schedule of infusion dates and any necessary pre-treatment bloodwork.
- Request an estimate of how long each session will take (the first session is usually longer).
- Know the chemo side effects you are likely to experience and discuss medications to help manage them.
- Ask about prescription medications you will need before and after chemo (anti-nausea, steroids, Claritin for bone pain, and other medications).

Plan Your Transportation

- Do not drive yourself to the first chemotherapy session; arrange for a ride.
- Consider having a designated driver for all treatments in case you are too tired or dizzy afterward.
- Keep a small vomit bag in the car, just in case.

Prepare Your Calendar

- Block off rest days after each chemo session; you will need recovery time.
- Schedule hair appointments if you plan to cut your hair short before it starts falling out.
- Set reminders to take pre-chemo medications if prescribed.

Get Lab Work Done on Time

- Chemo will not be administered if your blood counts are too low. Eating plenty of protein and staying hydrated can help support your blood counts between treatments.
- Hydrating well before blood draws makes veins easier to access.

Set Up Your Home

Food and Hydration

You will see 'hydration' mentioned several times in these lists. That is intentional because it matters that much.

- Prepare protein-rich meals in advance; your body needs protein to rebuild blood cells.
- Stock up on hydration drinks (Gatorade Zero, Pedialyte, electrolyte powders).
- Keep bland foods available in case of nausea (such as toast, crackers, applesauce, bananas, or rice).
- Buy plastic utensils; chemo can cause a metallic taste in your mouth, and metal utensils can make it worse.

Comfort Items

- Get a body pillow and a weighted blanket for extra support while resting.
- Buy a wedge pillow to help with nausea or acid reflux.
- Set up a cozy rest area with blankets, pillows, and all essentials nearby.
- Get a humidifier to prevent dry mouth and skin.

Household Help

- Arrange for cleaning help; even light chores will feel exhausting.
- Ask a neighbor to take out your trash cans on collection days.
- Plan for pet care. Who will feed, walk, or clean up after your pets if you are too tired?
- Set up grocery delivery or ask someone to shop for you.

Medications and Supplements

Ask Your Pharmacist about Drug Interactions

- Do not take supplements (vitamins, herbal remedies, probiotics) without discussing them with your doctor.

Some may interfere with chemo or reduce its effectiveness.

- Claritin (loratadine) may help with bone pain from Neulasta (a brand name for pegfilgrastim), which is given to support white blood cell recovery after chemo. Ask your oncologist.

- I found Peppermint Tums work best for chemo-related heartburn.

Stock Up on Over-the-Counter Medications

- Anti-nausea meds (if not prescribed, ask about over-the-counter options).
- Anti-diarrhea meds (Imodium) and BRAT diet foods. BRAT stands for Bananas, Rice, Applesauce, and Toast.
- Stool softeners or fiber supplements (chemo can cause constipation).
- Gentle toothpaste and mouthwash (alcohol-free to prevent mouth sores).
- Hard as Hoof nail cream to protect against brittle nails and bleeding cuticles.
- Steroid creams for skin sensitivity during radiation.

What to Pack in Your Chemo Bag

Chemo sessions can last several hours, so bring items to help you stay comfortable and pass the time.

Clothing and Comfort

- Wear loose, comfortable clothes (a zip-up hoodie, a V-neck, or a loose-fitting shirt for easy port access).
- Warm socks and a blanket; chemo rooms are often cold.
- Frozen gloves and socks; they help prevent neuropathy.

Snacks and Hydration

- Protein bars, nuts, fruit, or bland crackers for easy snacking.

- A large water bottle with a straw; drinking fluids helps your body flush chemo faster.
- Ginger candy or mints for nausea.

Entertainment and Distractions

- Noise-canceling headphones to block out beeping machines.
- Podcasts, audiobooks, Netflix downloads, or music playlists.
- A journal or notebook to jot down questions, symptoms, or thoughts.

Medical Essentials

- Lip balm and hand lotion; chemo dries out your skin.
- A small fan if you get hot flashes.
- A vomit bag in case nausea hits.
- Hand sanitizer. Hospitals and clinics are full of germs, and your immune system will be weakened.
- Your ID and insurance card. Many centers require them at check-in.
- A list of current medications and allergies, just in case.
- A small notebook with important numbers (pharmacy, oncologist, emergency contact).

More Comfort and Self-Care Items

- Cooling towel; some chemo drugs cause hot flashes or excessive sweating.
- Eye mask and earplugs; if you want to nap, these block out light and noise.
- Soft hair cap: if your hair is thinning but not yet gone, a soft cap keeps your head warm and comfortable.

Chemo-Specific Needs

- A small, soft pillow for arm support if the IV placement is uncomfortable.
- Chemo port numbing cream (if your doctor recommends it). Apply about 30 minutes before access.

Personal Motivation and Mindset

- A small inspirational note or picture, something meaningful to remind you why you are fighting.

- A gratitude journal, if writing helps you process your journey.
- A comfort item, such as a small stuffed animal, a worry stone, or something soothing.

Final Reminders before Your First Chemo Session

- Hydrate well the day before and the morning of treatment.
- Eat a good meal before chemo; it helps with energy and nausea.
- Take pre-chemo meds as prescribed (anti-nausea, steroids, Claritin if recommended).
- Have a ride arranged; do not drive yourself.
- Prepare for fatigue; block off time to rest after the treatment.
- Set expectations with family and work; you may need more downtime than you think.

Takeaway: Set Yourself Up for Success

Chemo is a marathon, not a sprint. Preparing in advance reduces stress, conserves energy, and makes treatment more manageable. Take it one step at a time and let people help you; you do not have to do this alone.

Plan Ahead for Chemo Recovery

Chemo does not end when you leave the infusion center. The next few days can bring fatigue, nausea, bone pain, brain fog, and a range of other side effects. It is essential to plan ahead to recover as comfortably as possible. This list is meant to empower you to take control of your post-chemo experience and minimize discomfort as much as possible.

Prioritize Rest and Recovery

- Give yourself permission to rest; your body does hard work, even when you are lying down.

- Nap as needed, but be mindful of too much daytime sleep, which may disrupt nighttime rest.

- Use a weighted blanket or body pillow to ease discomfort and help with sleep.

- Listen to your body. Some days you will have energy, and some days you will not.

Stay Hydrated and Nourished

- Drink plenty of water to help flush out the chemo drugs from your system.

- Electrolyte drinks (like Relyte, Liquid IV, or Pedialyte) can help if you feel weak or dehydrated.

- Eat small, frequent meals, even if you are not hungry. Keeping something in your stomach helps alleviate nausea.

- Prioritize protein intake; aim for one gram of protein per pound of body weight to support recovery.

- Have easy-to-digest foods ready. Smoothies, soups, oatmeal, and yogurt can be gentler on your stomach.

Manage Side Effects

- Take Claritin (if recommended by your doctor) a few days before and after chemo, to help reduce bone pain.

- Use Peppermint Tums; often this is the only flavor that helps with chemo-induced heartburn.

- Use alcohol-free mouthwash and a soft toothbrush to protect sensitive gums.

- Apply Hard as Hoof nail cream nightly to prevent brittle nails and cracked cuticles.

- Wear light gloves while sleeping after applying hand cream to help with dry, peeling skin.
- Keep vomit bags nearby just in case nausea hits suddenly. I found sleeping with a wedge to keep my head and torso higher helped keep the nausea at bay. As soon as I was lying flat, I was sick.

Prepare for Digestive Issues

- Have Imodium or anti-diarrheal medication on hand in case of unexpected fecal urgency.
- Consider wearing adult diapers if you need to be out of the house for long periods; many people experience sudden diarrhea with little warning.
- Use a wedge pillow to reduce acid reflux at night.

Manage Brain Fog and Fatigue

- Use a pillbox to keep track of medications; you may feel too mentally foggy to remember otherwise.
- Write down important reminders in a notebook or on your phone.
- Plan light activities such as taking short walks, listening to music, or watching uplifting shows, which can serve as good distractions.

Take Care of Your Skin and Body

- A warm shower or bath can help with muscle stiffness and joint pain.
- A shower chair can be helpful if you are too exhausted to stand.
- Apply gentle lotions to help with dry, itchy skin, especially if you are also going through radiation.
- Use recommended creams for radiation rashes.
- Pomade or curl cream can help manage regrowing hair as it comes back in different textures.

Lean on Your Support System

- Say yes to offers of help, whether it is meals, errands, or household chores.
- Connect with online support groups (like Reddit or Facebook groups) for tips and emotional support.
- Let people know what you need. Many people want to help, but do not know how.

Plan for the Next Round

- Track side effects; write down what you experience so you can talk to your doctor.
- Prepare your chemo bag again for the next infusion.
- Schedule something small to look forward to, even if it is a movie night or a favorite meal.

Once you have a sense of what you need and what helps you feel supported, the next step is helping the people around you understand how to show up. That is where the following guide comes in.

A Guide for Your Support Circles

Share this with your Inner Circle and ask that they share it with key people in your Middle and Outer Circles. (See Chapter 29 to read about *The Circle of Support.*)

Ways to Support Someone with Cancer

When someone you care about is diagnosed with cancer, it's natural to want to help, but knowing how to help can feel overwhelming. I learned firsthand how much of a difference small acts of kindness can make during a difficult time. Whether it's offering practical assistance or providing emotional support, what matters most is showing up in ways that feel meaningful to the person going through it. *I expand on these ideas in Section Four, where you'll find detailed checklists for friends, family, and caregivers.*

The advice here is based on my own experiences and those of others who've faced similar challenges. Every cancer journey is different, so approach your loved one with empathy, flexibility, and an open mind. Listen to their needs, respect their boundaries, and remember that even the smallest gestures can mean the world to them. *For more on what to say—and what not to say—see the caregiver communication guide in Section Four.*

1. Practical Help

- Drive them to appointments.
- Drop off meals (ask about preferences and dietary needs!)
- Set up a rotating schedule with other friends and family.
- Help with house chores (laundry, pet care, errands)
- Arrange grocery or meal delivery.

- Offer childcare or pet-sitting.
- Help with paperwork or medical forms.

2. Emotional Support

- Check in via text or call without expecting a reply.
- Send a care package with thoughtful gifts (soft socks, audiobooks, tea, journals)
- Be a good listener (let them talk without offering unsolicited advice)
- Remind them it's okay to rest and ask for help
- Respect their need for space on tough days

3. Thoughtful Gestures

- Gift a subscription to a streaming service, audiobook platform, or meditation application.
- Provide cozy items like socks, blankets, or care packages with tea, snacks, or journals.
- Arrange childcare or pet care to ease their responsibilities.
- Send gift cards for food delivery services or local restaurants.

What to Say (and What Not to Say)

What to Say

- "I'm here for you."
- "How can I support you?"
- "You're doing so well—I'm proud of you."
- "I'm at the supermarket. What can I pick up for you?"

What Not to Say (and Better Alternatives)

I've mentioned some of these already, but here is a more comprehensive list.

1. **"Let me know if you need anything."**

     o   **Why it's problematic:** This puts the burden on the patient to ask for help.

     o   **Better approach:** "I'm free Tuesday to drop off dinner or pick up groceries—would that work for you?"

2. **"My [friend/cousin/neighbor] had cancer and they..."**

     o   **Why it's problematic:** Sharing someone else's cancer story can be upsetting or irrelevant.

     o   **Better approach:** Focus on the patient: "I'm here for you and thinking of you."

3. **"Stay positive!"**

     o   **Why it's problematic:** This can dismiss their valid emotions, making them feel they must hide their struggles.

     o   **Better approach:** "I can't imagine how hard this must be, but I'm here to listen."

4. **"At least it's not [another type of cancer]" or "At least they caught it early."**

     o   **Why it's problematic:** Minimizing their diagnosis invalidates their experience.

     o   **Better approach:** "That sounds really tough. How are you feeling about everything?

5. **"Everything happens for a reason."**

   - ○ **Why it's problematic:** This can feel dismissive or conflict with their beliefs.

   - ○ **Better approach:** "I'm so sorry you're going through this."

6. **"You're so strong—you've got this!"**

   - ○ **Why it's problematic:** This can create pressure to always appear strong.

   - ○ **Better approach:** "I admire your strength, but it's okay to feel however you're feeling. I'm here for you."

7. **"Have you tried [unproven remedy]?"**

   - ○ **Why it's problematic:** Suggesting unverified treatments can be frustrating or undermine trust in their medical team.

   - ○ **Better approach:** Support their healthcare decisions without offering unsolicited advice.

8. **"You don't look sick."**

   - ○ **Why it's problematic:** This can invalidate the challenges they're facing.

   - ○ **Better approach:** "You're amazing for dealing with so much."

9. **"A positive attitude is the key to beating cancer."**

   - ○ **Why it's problematic:** This places undue responsibility on the patient's mindset.

   - ○ **Better approach:** "I'm rooting for you and here to help however I can."

10. **"How much time do you have?"**

- o **Why it's problematic:** This is invasive and focuses on the wrong thing.

- o **Better approach:** "How are you feeling today?"

When in doubt, listen more than you speak. Offering your presence, understanding, and practical help can mean more than trying to "fix" or cheer someone up. Ask open-ended questions like, "What can I do to make things easier for you?" Your compassion and care can make all the difference.

Practical Strategies for Living Forward

Cancer doesn't end on the last day of treatment. There's an *after* that can be even harder—physically, emotionally, mentally, and spiritually. Once the appointments slow down and the noise stops, you're left with the task of rebuilding your life piece by piece. Here's what helped me move forward when everything felt unfamiliar.

Emotional Resilience

1. **Acknowledge Your Feelings.**

   Check in with yourself daily. Write it down if that helps. Tracking what you can control (your routines, your rest, your boundaries) and what you can't (test results, timelines, other people's reactions) can bring clarity. Learn the emotional patterns that emerge after treatment: grief, fear, anger, confusion, and relief. None of them is wrong.

2. **Lean on Your Support System.**

   Talk to people who make you feel safe. That may be friends, family, a therapist, or a cancer counselor. The emotional whiplash after treatment is real. You do not have to carry it alone.

3. **Take Care of Your Body.**

   Eat consistently, move gently, sleep when you can. Walks, hydration, stretching, and sunlight helped me more than I expected. The body keeps the score—support it while it recalibrates.

Mindset Shifts

4. **Find the Light Where You Can.**

   Not toxic positivity — but real moments that remind you you're still here. During my knee injury, I had to focus on what I *could* still do. Cancer required the same mindset. If everything feels different now, give yourself permission to explore what your "new normal" might look like.

5. **Reconnect With Joy.**

   Return to hobbies, or find new ones that fit the energy you have now. Music, movies, reading, Pilates, painting, gardening—joy doesn't have to be big. Joy just has to be yours.

Action-Oriented Support

6. **Set Gentle, Realistic Goals.**

   Not the corporate kind. The human kind.

- Walk every morning before work.
- Try one new recipe a week.
- Schedule follow-up appointments on time.
- Practice asking for help without apologizing.
- Do something creative on Sundays.

Your goals after cancer are about rebuilding your life, not optimizing performance.

7. **Help Others When You're Able.**

You don't have to save the world. But sharing your story, answering a question in a support group, or simply telling someone, "I get it," can change everything for a person who feels alone. Helping others helped *me* heal.

8. **Stay Connected.**

One thing cancer teaches you is how isolating hard things can be. Reach out to people when you have capacity. A walk, a coffee chat, a laughter break — connection matters more after cancer than before.

Navigating Uncertain Times

This applies during treatment, after treatment, during surveillance, and honestly, anytime life knocks you sideways.

1. **Prepare for Sneaker Waves.**

Certain smells, doctor's offices, a song in a grocery store — something will hit out of nowhere and bring tears to your eyes. It's normal. Let the feelings come, and then let them move through.

2. **Find Ways to Contribute.**

Helping others creates meaning during recovery. Volunteer. Support a newly diagnosed friend. Share resources. Offer practical help. Contributions don't have to be big to matter.

3. **Clarify What Actually Matters Now.**

A cancer diagnosis rearranges priorities whether you want it to or not. Pay attention to what you have energy for—and what now feels draining, unimportant, or misaligned.

4. **Rest Without Apologizing.**

Your body is rebuilding. Your mind is recalibrating. Rest is not optional; rest is treatment.

5. **Ask Real Questions.**

Talk to your oncologist about what's normal, what's not, what to expect, and when to be concerned. Information calms fear. Clarity eases anxiety. If you're afraid to ask something, ask anyway.

6. **Focus Only on What You Can Control.**

Scan results will be what they are. Traffic will be traffic. Other people will react however they react. You get to choose how you spend your energy, who you let in, and how you care for yourself.

7. **Keep Learning About Yourself.**

Journaling, therapy, support groups, survivorship programs — anything that helps you understand your own patterns and needs is worth your time.

Chapter 36: Recommended Reading, Apps, Support Groups, and Resources

Books

When I had my **panic attack**, I found these two books helpful. They were both recommendations from my cancer psychologist.

> Harris, R. (2021). *When life hits hard: How to transcend grief, crisis, and loss.* New Harbinger Publications.
>
> Stuntz, E. C. (2021). *Coping with cancer: Dialectical Behavior Therapy (DBT) skills to manage your emotions and balance uncertainty with hope.* Guilford Publications.

This one was helpful when I found out I was going on the drug **Herceptin**.

> Bazell, R. (1998). *Her-2: The making of Herceptin, a revolutionary treatment for breast cancer.* Random House.

Podcasts

Many podcasts address breast cancer.
- *So Now I've Got Breast Cancer*
- *The Breast Cancer Podcast*
- *Investigating Breast Cancer*
- *Breast Cancer and the Unknown*
- *Upfront About Breast Cancer – What You Don't Know Until You Do*

Reddit Communities

For me, Reddit was a significant source of information and support. There is a group for patients called /breastcancer. You are encouraged only to post if you are a patient. You can lurk and read everything if you are a caretaker or partner. I learned a lot from researching and reading about other people's journeys, suggestions, and experiences. As I described what I felt one day, the other Redditors convinced me to go to the hospital. That's when I discovered I had a blood clot in my lungs.

If it were not for the online community, I probably would have delayed longer and jeopardized my recovery. I felt like I could not catch my breath, and an elephant was sitting on my chest. That was all the /breastcancer Redditors needed to hear to convince me to contact my doctor and go to the emergency room.

Facebook Groups

Other women have had great support from the Facebook group called "Breast Friends." Do a search and see what is available to you. I also used Facebook to learn about the drugs I was prescribed, what side effects to expect, and how to combat them.

Body Image & Sexuality Resources

While I chose to focus on hair loss and identity shifts in my own story, I know many people struggle with body image, intimacy, and sexuality during and after breast cancer. These are deeply personal and essential topics, and there are excellent resources that explore them further.

Resource	Description	Link
American Cancer Society – Body Image & Sexuality After Breast Cancer	Compassionate guidance to explore and accept body changes, manage side effects, and rebuild comfort with yourself.	https://www.cancer.org/cancer/types/breast-cancer/living-as-a-breast-cancer-survivor/body-image-and-sexuality-after-breast-cancer.html
Living Beyond Breast Cancer – LGBTQ+: Body Image, Sexuality & Family Planning	Articles and tools for LGBTQ+ people navigating intimacy, body acceptance, and family planning.	https://www.lbbc.org/lgbtq-plus/body-image-sexuality
National LGBTQI+ Cancer Network	National network supporting LGBTQ+ cancer patients with risk info, support services, and advocacy.	https://cancer-network.org/about/
Prevent Cancer Foundation – Male Breast Cancer Stigma	Explores body image and intimacy challenges faced by men with breast cancer.	https://preventcancer.org/article/male-breast-cancer-stigma/
Verywell Health – Personal Story: Male Breast Cancer Survivor	A firsthand account by a male survivor, exploring the emotional and social aspects of breast cancer.	https://www.verywellhealth.com/len-robertson-breast-cancer-story-5198218

Hospital Resources

Your nurses and navigators at the hospital can also connect you to additional groups and resources to help you. They gave me a large 3-ring binder with flyers and other information on the support available at the hospital. Some groups offer free house cleaning and rides to and from the hospital. There are many avenues to seek help.

Moving On

By now, you've heard my story, reflected on loss and renewal, listened to others' voices, and gathered practical tools for patients, caregivers, and workplaces. My hope is that this book has given you both recognition and direction—something that says, *"Yes, this is hard, and here's how we keep going anyway."*

Before we close, I want to leave you with a few final reflections. They aren't instructions or checklists. They're reminders—the truths I carry with me now, after treatment, after grief, after rebuilding. They're what I hold onto when fear creeps in or when I forget how far I've come.

This last section is less about cancer itself and more about living with what it teaches us: clarity, perspective, and the daily choice to focus on what matters most.

SECTION SEVEN

Journaling & Reflecting

❀ ❀ ❀ ❀ ❀ ❀ ❀

Chapter 37: Journaling as a Tool for Healing

When I was diagnosed, I found that I couldn't control much. I was told what the process would be based on the test results, and then where to go and what to do to eradicate the cancer inside me. Besides my reaction, the one thing I could control was writing about how I felt and being my own witness to my experience. My Facebook posts, scribbled notes, and even the messages I sent to close friends became a record of what I was living through. Writing helped me process fear, grief, and even the funny moments that cropped up along the way. It also helps me help others who may be early in their cancer journey.

You don't have to be a "writer" to keep a journal. Journaling is simply about giving yourself a safe place to tell the truth. That truth might come out in words, drawings, audio notes, or even short videos. It doesn't matter what form it takes; the act of getting it out of your head and into another space is what helps.

Why Journaling Matters

When we're in the middle of a crisis, thoughts can feel tangled, looping, or overwhelming. Journaling slows things down. It creates distance between the thought and the thinker. By capturing emotions in words or images, you give them form—and once they're on the page, they're easier to look at, examine, and release.

When I was recovering from my soccer accident and learning how to walk again, I found a blog board on Kneeguru for people with injuries like mine. Talking with family and friends wasn't helping; they couldn't relate to my experience. I felt alone. Sharing my story online, asking questions, and putting my words out there was both helpful and healing.

Through that journaling, I met John, a mountain biker who had wrecked his knee. We became pen pals and eventually started a Facebook group for others with multi-ligament knee injuries. We learned how rare we were—just a fraction of a percent of knee injuries involve more than one ligament and a dislocation—an exclusive club we didn't want to join. What mattered most wasn't the rarity but the connection. Writing about our pain and progress created a lifeline. I credit John and the group for helping me process and heal, one entry at a time.

The Science Behind Journaling

Researchers have studied expressive writing for decades. James Pennebaker and colleagues found that when people wrote about their deepest thoughts and feelings for 15–20 minutes over several days, they reported:

- reduced stress and anxiety,
- improved sleep,
- stronger immune function,
- greater clarity and meaning making (Pennebaker & Beall, 1986; Pennebaker, 1997).

More recent work shows that journaling can also reduce depressive symptoms, lower blood pressure, and improve emotional well-being for patients navigating trauma, chronic illness, and grief (Frattaroli, 2006; Ullrich & Lutgendorf, 2002).

Why does it work? Writing helps the brain organize and integrate difficult experiences. It transforms chaotic thoughts into a coherent narrative, enabling us to process and begin healing.

By keeping my journal on Facebook, I was able to count down the treatments and display the completion percentage to my readers and myself. This slow and steady progress made it easier to get from week to week. Logging my symptoms and tracking their improvement or worsening from week to week was also helpful. The doctors ask about what's going on in between infusions and treatments, and having it written down was helpful. My brain was getting foggier, but having recorded things in the moment really helped me hold on to my sanity.

Different Ways to Journal

Journaling doesn't have to look a certain way. Here are some different ways to journal.

- **Traditional writing**: Pen and paper in a notebook or journal.
- **Typing**: A computer document, a phone note, or even an email to yourself.
- **Voice recording**: Speaking your thoughts into your phone.
- **Video journaling**: Recording short clips to capture how you feel in the moment.
- **Creative journaling**: Sketching, collaging, or pasting in photos.
- **Bullet journaling**: Quick lists instead of long entries.
- **Prompted journaling**: Responding to a question when you feel stuck.

I am a traditional writer. I also enjoy typing since it's faster, and my handwriting is atrocious. I want to be able to read what I wrote. If I handwrite, there is a chance I won't be able to read it—and I won't be able to get all the ideas out because I am so much slower with a pen than with a keyboard. I didn't do any voice recordings for this part of my life; however, I have done them in the past. Usually, when I was in the car, something came to me that I didn't want to forget. I would call myself and leave a voicemail. When I was in high school, I kept a journal/diary and would include stickers, photos, and brochures. I have tried bullet journaling, and I haven't quite gotten the hang of it.

Prompts That Help

A blank page can feel intimidating. That's why I used prompts for myself, for the women who shared their stories in this book, and even for Gus, when he wrote his section. Prompts create a doorway into the story—they give you something to react to instead of starting from nothing.

Prompts for Patients

- What's weighing most heavily on me right now?
- What small thing brought me comfort today?
- If my body could speak, what would it say?
- What do I wish others understood about what I'm going through?
- Who or what is carrying me through?
- What would I tell someone newly diagnosed?

Prompts for Caregivers

- What was it like to hear the diagnosis as a partner or loved one?
- What's been the most challenging part of caregiving for me?
- What did I need that people didn't always give?
- What moments of connection or joy did I hold onto?
- What advice would I give another caregiver just starting this journey?

Prompts for Reflection Beyond Cancer

- What part of my old life do I miss most?
- What part of my new life surprises me?
- What am I learning about myself in this season?
- Where do I find joy when nothing feels joyful?

As you read my diary entries, the stories of other women, and my caregiving husband, you may notice that the responses came after the writer was prompted. If you don't know where to start, start with some of the questions above. See what comes out and where your writing takes you.

Journaling Together

When I invited other women to contribute their stories, I didn't just say, "Tell me what happened." That can feel overwhelming. Instead, I offered them prompts—gentle questions to help them find their way into the story. Each woman could choose which questions to answer and how deeply to go. Prompts created structure, and with structure came safety.

The same worked for Gus. As a caregiver, he wasn't sure where to begin, so the prompts gave him permission to tell his story in his own way.

When I was reading Gus's responses, I was surprised by his note that what saddened or surprised him most was that cancer was taking away what made me, me. That I couldn't do the things and behave the way he was accustomed. That was enlightening. I didn't know that before I asked him to write about his experience.

Tips for Beginners

- **Set a small goal**: Even five minutes counts.
- **Don't edit yourself**: Grammar and spelling don't matter.
- **Choose your time**: Mornings, evenings, or treatment days—find your rhythm.
- **Use prompts**: Let a question guide you when you're stuck.
- **Be honest**: Write the messy truth, not the brave version.

Remember: this is for you. No one else has to see it.

You don't need beautiful sentences—you just need honesty.

Write the truth. Write about your truth. Your questions. Your ideas. Your worries. Your joys. Your progress. You may be surprised by what ends up on the page.

Why It Matters

For me, journaling became a lifeline. On hard days, I could look back and see how far I'd come. On better days, I had proof of joy worth holding onto. For the women who shared their stories here, journaling gave them the courage to speak their truth. For Gus, it gave him a way to process his caregiving experience.

You don't need to start perfectly. Just start. Whether it's one sentence, a scribble, a voice note, or a quick video—it counts. Over time, those small moments build into something bigger: a record of survival, resilience, and healing. And it could also turn into a way to connect with others or help your family and friends understand your journey.

Chapter 38: Final Reflections: Living with What I've Learned

Cancer has taken plenty from me. But amid all that loss, it also brought some surprising gifts.

I already learned the lesson of who my friends were years ago, when I shattered my leg playing soccer. This time around, cancer validated those older friendships and brought new ones into my life with more frequency and purpose.

It also gave me smaller boobs. I don't know why it took cancer for me to get a breast reduction, but I'm so glad I did. Two years out, they've settled into a size and shape I love. The scars have faded, I can go braless when I want, and exercise is so much easier. Every woman who feels weighed down by her breasts deserves the chance to choose what fits her body and lifestyle.

Chemo even gave me a gift I didn't expect: clear skin. For two years, my rosacea all but disappeared. When it came back, I finally went back to the dermatologist. I discovered a new treatment (a miracle gel called Rovis) that has cleared my skin better than anything else I've ever tried. Without chemo giving me that glimpse that clear skin was possible, I might not have asked for help again. Healthcare and research are constantly changing. Keep asking, you never know what you'll find.

Most importantly, cancer sharpened my perspective on time. I try not to bemoan the past or worry about the future. Instead, I practice the "sphere of control" every day: What can I control? What can I influence? What's out of my control entirely? That simple framework has given me peace. My blood pressure is lower, I'm calmer, and I'm able to move through life more present and grounded. I don't dread scans and tests months in advance anymore. When the day comes, I'll deal with it. Everything in its time.

I know people who worry they'll get cancer one day. Here's the truth: you can't live in that fear. Illness is complicated, and so much of it is environmental. All we can do is make the best choices we can—eat well, move our bodies, don't smoke, don't inhale what we don't need to, drink in moderation—and then stay vigilant. Keep your annual physicals. Go to the dentist. See your eye doctor. Get the bump checked. Don't brush things off. Catching something early is the best chance we've got.

And then? Live. Fully. Look for the positive and kind things that happen each day. Share them with the people you love. Take photos. Celebrate the small moments. The more you look for joy, the more you'll find—and the easier it is to deal with the hard stuff when it comes.

Even in the car, I find myself calmer now. I remind myself I've got choices: slow down, go around, pull over, or just give them space. Most of the time, I choose peace. Being someone who is chronically early helps too.

And I know I'm not alone. Other women have shared their "good things" too: a new boldness, a stronger voice, a softer heart. Some quit smoking, some fell in love with their curly regrowth, some found new family members, and some discovered art. One woman crocheted a poncho to represent her journey. Another finally used her yarn stash. Another said simply, "It stripped away the last of my give-a-damns."

The good thing about cancer is that it strips life down to what matters. And once you know what matters, you stop wasting time on the rest.

None of us would have chosen this path. But here we are— living, learning, laughing where we can. Finding strength we didn't know we had.

If you've made it this far, thank you for being here with me. Writing this book was never about reliving the hardest days of my life—it was about making something useful out of them. If sharing my story inspires even one person to pick up the phone and schedule their mammogram, or to show up better for a friend who's going through cancer, then every word was worth it.

So please: take care of yourself. Make the appointment. Pay attention to your body. And if someone in your life is facing cancer, show up with love, patience, and presence. None of us should have to walk this road alone.

My wish for you is that you live fully, laugh often, and give your energy only to what matters most.

If cancer taught me anything, it's that we don't get to go back to who we were. We only get to become who we are now. I'm still a mother, a wife, a coach, a friend, a woman who lifts weights, a dog lover, a teacher, and someone who believes deeply in second chances. But I'm also different: steadier, quieter in the right ways, louder in the places that matter, and far more intentional with my time. I don't chase perfection anymore. I chase presence. And if this experience offered one lasting gift, it's this reminder: we get one life. One body. One moment at a time. Use it well. Love people well. And don't wait to start over when you need to. Start today.

SECTION EIGHT

Gratitude & Resources

✿ ✿ ✿ ✿ ✿ ✿ ✿ ✿

Acknowledgments

This book would not have been possible without the unwavering support of so many incredible people.

To my husband, **Gus**: You were my rock during the most challenging moments of this journey. Your strength, humor, and love grounded me when everything else felt uncertain. You balanced so much with grace, and I am endlessly grateful.

To my daughters, Julia and Claire: **Julia**, your research and thoughtful suggestions helped me navigate the overwhelming sea of information when I couldn't face it on my own. The /breastcancer Reddit community you introduced me to was an invaluable resource. **Claire**, your pragmatic and steadfast nature kept me grounded in the present. You both inspire me every day.

To my mom, **Valerie**, and my sister, **Ali**: Your listening ears, heartfelt advice, and undying support carried me through the darker days.

To my friends and family:

- **Talli:** Your texts, VR mini-golf sessions, and constant check-ins reminded me that I was never alone. You're the friend everyone deserves—especially during tough times.
- **Erin:** Your care package full of practical items—snacks, wooden utensils, and more—addressed problems I didn't even know I'd face. Thank you for your wisdom and foresight.
- **Sarah**, my dear former work-wife: You turned a traumatic experience—cutting my waist-length hair to a buzzcut—into a moment of care and courage.

You made the unbearable feel manageable.

- **Carrie, Michelle, Vicki, Gia, Teresa, Damon, Wendy, Lynn, Anu, Kathy, Orlando,** and many others: Your food deliveries, thoughtful gifts, and messages brought joy and comfort when I needed it most.
- **Ursula**, thank you for driving me to chemo nearly every week and giving Gus a well-deserved break.

To my medical team:

- **Dr. Johnson**, you combined science and compassion, singing me to sleep before placing my port and later removing the remains of my tumor. Your approach ensured we knew the chemo was working before surgery.
- **Dr. Michelle Lee**, your practical exercises helped me shift from panic to resilience. Your energy and ideas were a port in the storm of diagnosis and worry.
- **Dr. Phoebe Trubowitz**, for listening and adjusting when the chemo became overwhelming.
- **Colleen Taylor**, your acupuncture treatments alleviated my pain, stress, swelling, and insomnia.
- **Dr. Kyle Baltruch**, for asking me what I wanted, listening carefully, and following my instructions to the letter during plastic surgery. Thank you for helping me join the 'itty bitty titty committee.'
- **Dr. Misa Lee** for guiding me through radiation with clear explanations and support. The reminder that I had done all the things and needed to shift into getting back to living was wonderfully helpful.

To my physical recovery team:

- My personal trainer, **Brett Ball,** ensured I built strength safely and consistently.
- The instructors at Club Pilates West Hills—**Michelle L., Michelle D., CJ, and Lori**—your adaptations and guidance helped me maintain mobility and avoid complications.
- **Abby**, my physical therapist at St. Vincent's, helped me regain balance despite the neuropathy in my hands and feet.

To the dogs who brought me smiles and solace, especially **Dakota**.

To **Aurora, Erin H., Gail, Shelby, and Vivian**, the amazing women who shared their stories: Your honesty and courage enriched these pages. Thank you for trusting me with your experiences, so that others may find comfort and guidance.

To my readers: Whether you are navigating your own diagnosis, supporting a loved one, or simply seeking to understand, thank you for engaging with these stories. Your willingness to listen, learn, and empathize means more than I can express.

Finally, to the countless women who face breast cancer every day: This book is for you. Together, we are stronger.

About the Author

Vikki Espinosa, CPC, is a career strategist, speaker, and breast cancer survivor dedicated to helping others navigate life's biggest challenges. After decades of coaching professionals through career transformations, she faced an unexpected reinvention—one shaped by  chemotherapy, resilience, and the rediscovery of strength in the face of illness.

A former parafencer for Team USA, Vikki has never been one to back down from a challenge. When breast cancer disrupted her retirement plans, she applied the same grit and determination she once used in competition to reclaim her health and advocate for herself in the medical system. Now, through *One in Eight*, she shares her story with the hope of empowering others, offering tactical advice, raw honesty, and a dose of humor along the way.

As life moves forward, Vikki is embracing a new chapter. She has returned to work, supporting students at Portland State University while pursuing her master's in education. Committed to helping others through life's most challenging transitions, she now mentors and supports other women undergoing cancer treatment, paying forward the wisdom, comfort, and hard-earned lessons of her own journey.

Vikki lives in the Pacific Northwest with her husband, Gus, and their two adult daughters, Julia and Claire. She finds joy in early-morning Pilates, long walks with her rescue dog, Georgie, and baking far more cookies than necessary.

When she's not coaching or writing, you'll find her lifting weights—defying chemo-induced osteoporosis one rep at a time.

You can connect with Vikki, explore her blog, and learn more about her journey at **vikkiespinosa.com**.

The Dogs Who Carried Me Through

The dogs are definitely not an afterthought. For those who don't appreciate or haven't had the privilege of living with dogs, I've moved this section to the back of the book. However, these wonderful pups played a vital role in my cancer journey, offering comfort, laughter, and unconditional love. Below are their stories:

Dakota – Our sweet rescue terrier mix, who looked like a gray and white Muppet. When we first got him, he was eight, and we had to pull all his teeth due to prior neglect. For his final years, I cooked for him because of his allergies. He passed away during my first round of chemo.

Georgie – Our energetic rescue from Bakersfield. She's a mix of eight breeds, with Chihuahua, Rat Terrier, and Poodle being the strongest. Georgie came from a hoarding situation and was rescued with twelve of her family members. She keeps us laughing and active with her boundless energy.

Gerber and Daisy – A pair of Chihuahuas who belong to a friend of a friend. With her long, skinny legs, Daisy was ancient and not very mobile. She passed away earlier this year. Middle-aged and stout, Gerber loves sneaking into bed with us at 2:30 a.m. Her antics always make us laugh.

Pippin – A gorgeous cream-colored retriever with the loudest bark in the neighborhood. He loves basking in the sun or playing fetch (but never brings the toy back). He adores everyone he meets.

Koda – A Bernese Mountain Dog who lived next door with our dear neighbors, Kathy and Orlando. During my treatment, he was slowing down due to age. He has since passed, but will always be remembered as the sweetest big dog ever. (Yes, he's the one in the photo.)

Lola – A Bernedoodle who joined our friends Carrie and Dutch this year. She brings so much joy to their lives. She is young, energetic, and cute as a stuffed toy.

Tapioca (Tapi) – Our first foster dog, a 10-year-old Chihuahua mix. Quiet and sweet, she was fearful of men. She now lives with a wonderful woman in Washington and has an adopted dog brother, Roo.

Ozzie – Our second foster dog. A Cockapoo with a touch of Chihuahua on top, Ozzie is as sweet as pie. He now lives with a loving couple in Washington and his sister dog, Ellie.

Book Club Guide: One in Eight

1. Vikki shares how her diagnosis shifted her sense of control and identity. How did this part of her story resonate with your own experiences of uncertainty or change?
2. What role did humor and lighthearted moments play in Vikki's journey? How do you use humor in your own hard times?
3. Several chapters explore the importance of support networks, including family, friends, and coworkers. What stood out to you about what was most (or least) helpful?
4. The book blends memoir with practical advice. Which sections felt most useful to you personally? Which do you think would help someone you know?
5. Vikki writes candidly about moments of vulnerability—panic attacks, fear, and body image. Did reading these moments shift your perspective on strength or resilience?
6. What is one takeaway from the book you'd like to carry into your own life—or share with others?

For an expanded Book Club Guide—including bonus questions, tips for hosting, and resources for caregivers, workplaces, and survivors, along with a Leader Script, visit:

vikkiespinosawrites.com/pages/book-club.

References

American Cancer Society. (2023). *Breast cancer facts & figures 2023-2024*. American Cancer Society. https://www.cancer.org/research/cancer-facts-statistics/breast-cancer-facts-figures.html

Bazell, R. (1998). *Her-2: The making of Herceptin, a revolutionary treatment for breast cancer*. Random House.

Cancer Center. (n.d.). *Breast cancer in men: Symptoms, risk factors, and treatment*. Retrieved December 30, 2024, from https://www.cancercenter.com

Cancer Therapy Advisor. (2024). *Breast cancer statistics for men and women*. Retrieved December 30, 2024, from https://www.cancertherapyadvisor.com

Centers for Disease Control and Prevention. (2023). *Breast cancer statistics*. Retrieved September 18, 2025, from https://www.cdc.gov/breast-cancer/statistics

Harris, R. (2021). *When life hits hard: How to transcend grief, crisis, and loss with acceptance and commitment therapy*. New Harbinger Publications.

Harter, J. (2023, July 6). *Leaders: Ignore employee wellbeing at your own risk*. Gallup. https://www.gallup.com/workplace/507974/leaders-ignore-employee-wellbeing-own-risk.aspx

Komen. (n.d.). *Breast cancer facts and statistics: Male breast cancer*. Retrieved December 30, 2024, from https://www.komen.org

Miserandino, C. (2003). *The spoon theory*. But You Don't Look Sick. https://butyoudontlooksick.com/articles/written-by-christine/the-spoon-theory

Mohr, T. (2014). *Playing big: Practical wisdom for women who want to speak up, create, and lead*. Avery.

National Breast Cancer Foundation. (n.d.). *Breast cancer facts*. Retrieved December 30, 2024, from https://www.nationalbreastcancer.org

National Cancer Institute. (2019). *Male breast cancer: Higher mortality compared to women*. Retrieved December 30, 2024, from https://www.cancer.gov

National Cancer Institute. (2023). *SEER cancer stat facts: Female breast cancer*. Surveillance, Epidemiology, and End Results Program (SEER). U.S. National Institutes of Health. https://seer.cancer.gov/statfacts/html/breast.html

National Comprehensive Cancer Network. (2025). *NCCN Clinical Practice Guidelines in Oncology (NCCN Guidelines®): Breast Cancer* (Version 4.2025). https://www.nccn.org/professionals/physician_gls/pdf/breast.pdf

Nepo, M. (2000). *The book of awakening: Having the life you want by being present to the life you have*. Conari Press.

Pennebaker, J. W. (1997). *Opening up: The healing power of expressing emotions*. New York: Guilford Press.

Pennebaker, J. W., & Beall, S. K. (1986). Confronting a traumatic event: Toward an understanding of inhibition and disease. *Journal of Abnormal Psychology, 95*(3), 274–281. https://doi.org/10.1037/0021-843X.95.3.274

Silk, S., & Goldman, B. (2013, April 7). *How not to say the wrong thing*. Los Angeles Times. https://www.latimes.com/opinion/story/la-timeless/how-not-to-say-the-wrong-thing

Stuntz, E. C. (2021). *Coping with cancer: DBT skills to manage your emotions and balance uncertainty with hope*. Guilford Publications.

U.S. Department of Labor. (2023). *Fact sheet #28: The Family and Medical Leave Act* (Wage and Hour

Division Publication No. 1421). U.S. Department of Labor. https://www.dol.gov/agencies/whd/fact-sheets/28-fmla

U.S. Equal Employment Opportunity Commission. (n.d.). *Cancer in the workplace and the ADA.* https://www.eeoc.gov/laws/guidance/cancer-workplace-and-ada

U.S. Food and Drug Administration. (2024). *Herceptin (trastuzumab) prescribing information.* https://www.accessdata.fda.gov/drugsatfda_docs/label/2024/103792s5354lbl.pdf